W9-ARI-886

.M54
1981

The Case for Liberal Christianity

DONALD E. MILLER

1817

Harper & Row, Publishers, San Francisco

Cambridge, Hagerstown, New York, Philadelphia
London, Mexico City, São Paulo, Sydney

Library of Congress Cataloging in Publication Data

Miller, Donald Earl.
THE CASE FOR LIBERAL CHRISTIANITY.

Includes index.
   1. Liberalism (Religion)   I. Title.
BR1615.M54 1981   230'.044   80-8355
ISBN 0-06-065753-7

81 82 83 84 85 10 9 8 7 6 5 4 3 2 1

Contents

To the community of A.S.C.

Preface

THIS BOOK is concerned with the problem of achieving a Christian identity in the modern world. It is written from the perspective of one who is personally a liberal Christian, an Episcopalian to be more precise, and one who is, by profession, a sociologist of religion. As the first chapter indicates, this book was, in part, born out of a personal attempt to define a Christian identity. It was also written, however, as a declaration about what I believe to be the task of the liberal church in a highly complex and pluralistic urban context.

Following the opening chapter, in which I chronicle (I hope not narcissistically) my own pilgrimage of faith, I argue a case for how the liberal Christian might think about the "truth" of his or her faith commitment. In this second section, I attempt to describe the truth claims of the Christian faith in terms of an understanding of the psychological and sociological dynamics surrounding religious experience and commitment. In the third section of the book, I examine the process of constructing a Christian identity in the modern world. This section emphasizes the importance of constructing that identity within a *community* of faith. My sociological bias shows at this point. The final section of the book offers a critique of several cultural trends within contemporary society, specifically the embrace by many persons of both a secular and a therapeutic mentality. The book ends with an examination of the possible complementarity between theological and social-scientific explanations of religious truth and commitment—but only after noting that psychological and sociological interpretations of religious experience probably pose the most serious contemporary threat to the Christian faith.

This book addresses three audiences. First, but

not in order of priority, it is directed toward those who have dropped out of the Christian church because they believe such a commitment is intellectually indefensible and, hence, have withdrawn their participation as an act of conscience. Second, I wish to address those individuals who are seeking a well-traveled pathway to meaning and truth, but who have yet to find an adequately rich and complex road on which to pursue the journey of faith. I believe that the Christian liberal tradition provides such a path. And third, the book is intended for clergy and religious educators on whose shoulders rests the task of providing a context within which Christian identity may be nurtured.

Yet an author may write for specific individuals, as well as for an abstract audience. A number of the thoughts in this book were provoked by discussions with my fishing partner and friend, Bruce Crapuchettes. Bill Pickering has at many points been a compatriot in the faith and a foil for my ideas. John P. Crossley, Jr., a colleague at the University of Southern California, read almost all of the chapters in rough draft form and more than once challenged me on positions I was assuming. I owe a great deal to John B. Orr, my primary mentor during graduate education, and to J. Wesley Robb, who was responsible for getting me involved in the academic study of religion. And I traded more than one idea in this book during the commute from Pasadena to Los Angeles with my car-pool mate and colleague, Robert S. Ellwood, Jr.

There is no way that I can adequately acknowledge the challenging and nurturing presence of my wife, Lorna, during eleven years of marriage. My children, Shont and Arpi, are an unremitting source of distraction and joy in my life. And to All Saints Church in Pasadena, to its people and staff, I dedicate this book. It was in this community that I experienced many of the ideas which follow.

INTRODUCTION

The Journey of Faith—Personal Reflections

1

INCREASINGLY I sense in myself, and in many individuals I encounter, an emerging new basis for commitment to the church and the Christian heritage. By any orthodox standard, this basis is heretical. But then, that is exactly where many of us find ourselves today: in a state of disbelief, struggling for some constructive way to make sense of our experiences.

The syndrome is well known: active religious upbringing, postadolescent crisis of faith, dubious commitment to the church—and then? What happens to those of us who go through a genuine intellectual crisis with respect to the primary articles of the Christian faith? Must the conclusion be that we have no rightful place in the Christian church, that we should drop out?

PURSUING THE JOURNEY OF FAITH

Reflecting upon my own experience, I strongly suspect that few persons experience a crisis of belief only to revert to their prior faith, experiencing it again in basically the same way as they did previously. Consciousness is progressive and cumulative; as our stock of experiences increases, the filter through which we view the world changes.[1] Although some may be able to strip away those layers of the filter associated with a waning faith, most of us have no choice but to press forward, placing new transparencies on the prism, hoping that the light (the

Spirit?) can still filter through. In short, from my perspective, the only way back to faith is to continue the journey forward, bringing new frames of reference to bear on our experience.

That statement may sound like a truism. It was born in part, however, out of my own futile attempt to "recover" a lost faith by *willing* that it reappear. This exercise of will included considerable hours spent reading and studying the Bible, praying, and immersing myself in apologetic defenses of the faith. These activities were by no means unimportant, but I had to conclude finally that one's convictions about things ultimate lie largely outside the realm of rational or willful control. For example, one either trusts a person, or believes in an aspect of the creed, or one does not. Intellectual arguments are pursued most often after the fact, to bolster and rationalize what one has already come to feel and believe on more intuitive and emotive grounds. Stated theologically, faith is a *gift* of God.[2]

My inability to return to the place where I had been before convinced me of the futility of a purely rational approach to the enterprise of attaining faith. It appeared that, short of hypnotic regression, there was no way to block out my intellectual and experiential journeys of the preceding ten years. The only direction was forward. Significantly, despite my questioning of the literal character of many theological affirmations, part of my emergent experience was a growing conviction that there is indispensable value in being a part of the Christian community and in participating regularly in the life of the church.

Though I gave up trying to mandate my feelings and coerce myself into certain beliefs, there was one measure of willful behavior I maintained. That was the decision to continue to participate regularly in the sacrament of Holy Communion as an expression of my desire to pursue the journey of faith. I suppose this "beliefless obedience" sprang from the realization that, though I could not control my feelings of belief, I could at least exercise some control over my behavior: regular attendance at worship services was a highly tangible way of indicating to myself the seriousness of my own engagement with the questions of ultimate meaning.

AFFIRMING THE COMMUNITY

Presently I find myself inalterably committed to the Christian community, its heritage, and the Spirit that energizes it. In the past decade, however, there has been a significant change in the way I approach my tradition. The issue no longer is what "really happened" some two thousand years ago. I believe there are more profound questions with which to concern oneself. I have given up on trying to settle the question of the resurrection, whether Jesus was born of a virgin, whether he made the blind see and the lame walk. The first-century community asserted that these events took place, but to me they remain—as historical happenings—somewhat enigmatic. Unlike Rudolf Bultmann, I possess no magic telescope to look back and say what really did *not* happen.[3] I remain agnostic, but open, on these issues of faith. In fact, I am more intolerant of those who from some early Enlightenment view of science exclude the supernatural than I am of those who say that on the basis of their experience in the Christian community they affirm the miraculous.[4]

I presently feel comfortable reciting the creed without editing it or feeling a pang of conscience if I affirm something that I do not literally believe—an act that once would have struck me as lacking integrity. Questions of historical interpretation, such as the resurrection of Jesus, no longer seem to me to be the watershed issues in Christianity. It is one thing for the Apostle Paul to say that either Christ rose from the dead or all is in vain. For me to make the same affirmation—twenty centuries and several world views removed from the event—is quite another thing. And yet it seems important to me regularly to recite that statement in the creed:

> He suffered death and was buried.
> On the third day he rose again
>   in accordance with the Scriptures;
> he ascended into heaven
>   and is seated at the right hand of the Father.

This is a statement of my history, of the tradition that has united my community—the Christian community—for twenty centuries. Wanting to be a part of that community of faith, I recite the creed, thereby affirming my commitment to the community.

The change in my thinking over the last decade is that meaning can function on more than one level. My postadolescent crisis of faith was the result of learning to read on only one level. Through sixteen years of schooling I was indoctrinated to believe that things were either true or false; they either happened or did not happen. When this type of reasoning is applied to a sacred text, one is placed in the awkward position of having to either affirm the whole thing or selectively deny it on very tenuous grounds, such as the fragility of one's present world view.

REFLECTING ON OUR ROOTS

To try to ascertain "what really happened" in those events we celebrate as Easter, Pentecost, and Christmas seems a futile endeavor. The only thing we will ever know with some certitude is what the early church understood as the basis for its community. Reality is always a social construction—in the fifth century B.C., the first century A.D., or the twentieth century. Furthermore, reality is always a *personal* construction—which is to say that meaning is constituted retrospectively as we direct our attention back to events that have elapsed in the stream of consciousness or the course of history. Meaning is a matter of interpretation, of bringing one's present frame of reference to bear on the events of the past.[5]

In the present, what events do we have to reflect upon? Only those we have experienced in our own community of faith and those presented to us by our predecessors as they reflected on their experience in the community. The Synoptic Gospels were not written until some thirty years or so after Jesus' death: which is to say, the first century Christian community had a number of years to mull over the meaning of Christ's life before it was recorded.[6]

What, then, are the creeds—or for that matter, the Scriptures? These documents are landmarks representing how those within the community of faith have reflected on the meaning of Christ for them and how they have struggled through the issues of community in their own time. They are statements of our past, of our forebears, of our roots. To recite the creed is to affirm one's tradition. Regularly reading the Scriptures reminds us whence we have come. These acts serve to keep alive the tradition. Why? Because it is in the tradition that we find the symbolic forms, the collective sentiments, which bind us together as a distinctive community that offers one a unique identity. In my changed understanding of the church's central affirmations, Scripture and creeds need not be viewed as metaphysical statements; rather, they are affirmations of the Christian community at a particular moment in time. The various creeds represent milestones in the history of my tradition. Likewise, the writings of the New Testament are historical documents reflecting the spirit of the Christian community at the time they were written. By taking a sociological frame of reference to one's understanding of the Bible and the creedal formulations of the church, one avoids getting into the divisive and irresolvable difficulties of deciding what is true in some ultimate, uncontaminated, pristine sense. Let us face the fact, and face it honestly, that we cannot turn back the clock of history to recover the historical Jesus. We are stuck with the early church's affirmation of the *meaning* which his life had for that community.

RITUAL ACTS

Over the last decade I have slowly been outgrowing my sophomoric, perhaps even "freshmanic," notion of truth as something that can be described in purely rationalistic terms. I have not lost my vision that a pure and ultimate Truth may exist. In fact, I suspect it does—our only problem as mortals is our perception of it. What I have come to realize is that my personal vision of the Truth is always going to be adulterated. Whatever else the Bible is, it is at least, as William James expressed it, the record of "great souled individuals wrestling with their fate."[7] Surely the creeds are the same thing. As for me, I am trying in some small measure to follow in the footsteps of those individuals, however imperfectly, and struggling to know the meaning of birth, death, suffering, success, failure, and purpose *in my time.*

The creeds have taken on a new significance for me—not so much as statements of what really happened, or of what will happen, but as sociological statements about the integrity of my tradition. To recite the creeds is to recall my heritage, my roots.

To take Holy Communion is to rehearse a significant event in the life of my community—the celebration of which throughout history has been absolutely central to the life of that community and to the experience of the Spirit that empowers it. To recite a creed, to participate in the Eucharist, to read Scripture, to sing hymns—all of these are ritual acts. The new day that has dawned for me and, I suspect, increasingly for others—despite the Protestant suspicion of ritual—is the realization that truth is somehow embodied in ritual and the other collective acts of the community. Ritual in itself is not sacred—this much we have gained from the Protestant Reformation—but rite and ritual are the *carriers* of truth. And in the collective acts of the community are to be found "new life."

The agnostic, nineteenth century French sociologist Emile Durkheim said that ritual provides the moment for "moral remaking." It is the time to celebrate, in his terms, the "collective sentiments"—those commonly held beliefs that describe the basis of community. For Durkheim, it is only in collective celebration that individuals become fully conscious of their commitment to the corporate group and to the spirit that energizes it.[8] And regarding the Spirit: I am not precluding its presence for the Christian, although I suspect that the Holy Spirit was certainly given at least as much to the community as to the individual Christian.

A POINT OF STABILITY

The positive aspect related to the temporary loss of faith is that this experience gives one a chance to look around at alternative meaning systems, their corresponding moral communities, and the options they pose to Christianity. Humanism, Marxism, psychoanalysis, nihilism, Zen—all have their limitations. The Christian community's competition is not bereft of difficulties; thus, perhaps, Christianity's ambiguities become a bit more tolerable. The central insight for me in reassociating myself with the Christian community has been the realization that what I was looking for was not just a belief system, but an identity or, more broadly stated, a tradition in which I could locate myself. I was looking for an identity that had more permanence than the titles associated with my job, nationality, and family roles. Furthermore,

I wanted (almost desperately) an identity with transcendent and metaphysical overtones.

In retrospect, my return to the church has been, I think, an attempt to find a community in whose membership I can find a point of stability and permanence. Indeed, the whole movement back to a commitment to the church started to make more sense when I reread Erik Erikson's discussion of identity as being tied to the discovery of an ideology, a belief system, that gives one a transcendent fix on the meaning and purpose for existence. Also illuminating is Erikson's observation that the problem of identity is solved often only after a "moratorium period," during which time one may do considerable wandering and sample various possibilities before settling on the ideology that will serve to unify one's life-style and moral commitments.[9]

Durkheim also was important to me in clarifying the point that ideologies are born in community and maintained there through regular rehearsal of those events that provide the symbolic paradigms through which members of the community understand themselves and their collective purpose. To claim identity as a "Christian" is to align oneself with a community whose symbolic forms have enabled that community to deal creatively with the social, psychological, and ethical dilemmas of many generations. To disavow my identity as a Christian would be to raise the precarious question: Who am I—morally, psychologically, spiritually?

One thing that brought me back to the church was asking simply: What are the alternatives to the church? Where are the communities that sanction the pursuit of meaning and truth as a legitimate enterprise? that have material and personal resources to assist in this search? that renew and inspire? that provide a setting where children are nurtured? where family members can be buried? where births can be celebrated? where social issues can be debated? There are a number of institutions that deal with one or several of these questions, but historically the church has demonstrated its ability to energize all of these activities.

I foresee an emerging membership in Christian churches of those for whom theological interpretations are undergoing important transformations. These are persons who recognize the ultimate emptiness of individualism, who seek membership in a community united by a common symbolic paradigm. They are those who want roots that can be celebrated collectively. They are those who have not given up the search for ultimate Truth, but who in all likelihood have concluded that truth is embodied only in community and is expressed and made available to individuals in the collectively celebrated rites, acts, and service of the community.

NOTES

1. My understanding of consciousness is heavily indebted to the thought of Alfred Schutz. For a complex but rewarding survey of many of his central ideas, see Alfred Schutz, *The Phenomenology of the Social World*, trans. George Walsh and Frederick Lehnert, with intro. by George Walsh (Evanston, Ill.: Northwestern University Press, 1967). For a more introductory volume, see Alfred Schutz, *On Phenomenology and Social Relations: Selected Writings*, ed. (with intro. by) Helmut R. Wagner (Chicago: University of Chicago Press, 1970).
2. I suspect that there is more Calvinism in my argument than I might want to admit. Or if it is not John Calvin, then perhaps it is Karl Barth. On one level, the initiative for divine illumination rests with God, not man; on a purely human level, the religious quest may net nothing more than a mirror reflection of oneself. I have been deeply influenced by Barth's slim volume *Evangelical Theology*, trans. Grover Foley (Garden City, N.Y.: Doubleday, Anchor Books, 1964), esp. pp. 140–184.
3. For a concise statement of Bultmann's position, see Rudolf Bultmann et al., *Kerygma and Myth: A Theological Debate*, ed. Hans Werner Bartsch (New York: Harper & Row, 1961), pp. 1–44.
4. On the relationship between science and religion, see Harold K. Schilling, *The New Consciousness in Science and Religion* (Philadelphia: Pilgrim Press, 1973); for a rather different perspective, see W. T. Stace, *Religion and the Modern Mind* (Philadelphia: J. B. Lippincott, 1952).
5. See Schutz, *Phenomenology of the Social World*, p. 69 ff.
6. On the controversy of dating the Synoptics, see John A. T. Robinson, *Redating the New Testament* (London: S.C.M. Press, 1976).
7. William James, *The Varieties of Religious Experience: A Study in Human Nature* (New York: Collier Books, 1961), p. 24.
8. See Emile Durkheim, *The Elementary Forms of the Religious Life*, trans. Joseph Ward Swain (Glencoe, Ill.: Free Press, 1947), p. 240 ff.
9. See Erik Erikson, *Young Man Luther: A Study in Psychoanalysis and History* (New York: W. W. Norton, 1958), pp. 99–100 ff.

COMMITMENT
BEYOND BELIEF

II

Truth Within Human Forms

2

FOR AT least a decade, liberal Christianity has been in decline—if membership and church attendance figures may serve as an index—while conservative churches have shown steady growth rates. Dean Kelley argues that the explanation for the difference between liberal and conservative churches is that conservative churches are demanding of their members, in terms of strictness both of belief and life-style, while liberal churches are pluralistic and open-minded, demanding little conformity. In Kelley's formula, *concept* plus *demand* equals *meaning*—with demand being of perhaps more importance than the content of what is being demanded.[1]

While there may be some limited value to Kelley's thesis, I do not believe the generalization holds that if liberal churches would only adopt the strictures of conservative Christianity, they would reverse their decline. The problem is more complex than Dean Kelley's explanation allows. I believe that the decline in liberal churches is related, at least in part, to the fact that the members of liberal churches are more integrated into the mainstream of secular American culture than are members of conservative churches. The result is that they are more affected by their experience in a pluralistic culture. The consequence of this experience is a relativizing of the Christian paradigm—and added demands for strictness of doctrine by the liberal clergy will not reverse the situation. For one reason, the clergy have their own difficulties with many traditional doctrinal interpretations. Hence, the decline of liberal churches is in large part the result of a crisis in the legitimating power of the Christian story as traditionally recited.[2]

In all likelihood, individuals who drop out from a liberal church may ostensibly identify their church's stand on some political or institutional issue as their reason for departure, but, in fact, the incident prompting their decision is only the *occasion* for their leaving. The precondition or contributing *source* of the problem is a more fundamental crisis in the way in which they conceptualize God, the church, prayer, and so on. Furthermore, the problem is compounded by the fact that many liberal ministers also, as part of the educated elite, are in an intellectual quandary. While they don't really believe the way their more conservative brethren do, many have not clearly articulated an alternative position. Such will be my task in this and the following two chapters: to articulate the reasonableness of a thoroughgoing liberal option.

My argument is not addressed to those who feel comfortable in their faith, who read the Bible regularly—believing it literally— and who pray with no difficulty. Rather, my concern is directed to those who contemplate prayer with troubled spirits (wondering what kind of psychological trick they may be playing on themselves), who try to read the Bible (but question Paul's exclusive right to interpret the meaning of Jesus' life), and who seek an all-embracing identity as a "Christian" (but realize how divided are their loyalties).

FORM AND SUBSTANCE

I part company with many in the evangelical camp not on pietistic grounds, but on epistemological grounds. Many of those of the "born-again" persuasion believe that Reality is identical with the written text of Scripture and that salvation comes through assent to a set of doctrinal statements.[3] In contrast to the literalism of such individuals, I must confess to having been influenced heavily by the social sciences in my interpretation of how meaning systems are created and evolve; although I view the New Testament writings as foundational to Christian faith and practice, I see them also as social constructions which are the natural by-products of a community's struggle with questions of meaning and faith. Furthermore, I do not regard God or Ultimate Reality as identical with the creedal statements or liturgical forms of which we are heirs.

Having stated these reservations, I nonetheless assert that Christianity is *true.* I believe it is true despite the fact that I simultaneously see our conceptualizations of Jesus and God, and the liturgical forms with which we celebrate their presence within our community of faith, as the *creative products* of individuals wrestling with their own fate.

What may sound paradoxical in my affirmation—namely, that Christianity is both true and a product of human creativity—can be clarified by making a distinction between "form" and "substance." The form which theological expression takes is always that of symbol and metaphor. As literal forms, these symbols and metaphors are social constructions, or one might say "social fictions."[4] God is never identical with an image or conceptualization. To identify the form of theological expression as fictional does not, however, discount the substance, or reality, to which these forms may point. The power of a theological "fiction" is its transparency to the reality it portrays. The literalist's mistake is to think that form and substance are one and the same. Distinguishing between form and substance enables one to recognize the human element in the social construction of religious expression without denigrating the reality of that which is encountered in religious experience.

THE REIFICATION PROCESS

Religious doctrine attempts to articulate the nature and character of the Ultimate Mystery, but it always falls short. Why? Because theology is the product of finite beings engaged in a reflective process that is *always* tempered by the limitations of the intellect at work. The best that the Christian theologian can hope for is to contribute to the comprehension of that one, Jesus, who was most transparent to the Ultimate. Jesus, as he is presented in the New Testament, is no less a symbolic form than the other social constructions which have emerged from the genius of individuals within the Christian community.[5] To say this is not to discount his historical reality—just as I do not discount the assertion that substance may underlie form—but it is to say that reality, on whatever level, is always conceptualized from the perspective and interests of the individual.[6]

Where religious communities (and individuals) go awry is in forgetting the human, and therefore finite and limited, authorship of all conceptualizations of the Ultimate. Reification is that process by which an abstraction or approximation comes to be treated as a concrete reality.[7] Doctrines and creeds are in their origin a product of human imagination. The historical tendency, however, is to forget that they are mere conceptualizations and to see them as being identical with reality itself.

The doctrine of the inspiration of Scripture is a good example of the reification process. At the time of writing, the authors of the biblical text surely were never audacious enough to believe that they were uttering Holy Writ. They were writing letters to friends, offering churchly counsel, constructing biographical accounts, or fashioning interpretations to make sense of what they had experienced.

It was only after some historical distance had been reached that a doctrine of verbal inspiration, for example, could arise. (At a time when individuals were haggling over which books should make it into the canon, it would have been laughable to argue the line taken by some fundamentalist literalists—that every word is inspired by God. And theologians as notable as Martin Luther later raised arguments as to whether the early councils had indeed chosen rightly in what they had included and excluded.) To "humanize" the biblical texts by pointing to their human authorship is not to discount their importance as the foundational documents on which the church stands, but such an approach does remove the idolatrous authority with which the words are sometimes stamped, thus acknowledging their social and historical rootedness.

FICTION AND MYTH

For modern individuals who are the intellectual heirs of Immanuel Kant, the Romantics, and the Enlightenment, the mind is better imaged as a lamp than as a mirror. A mirror reflects reality *as it is;* such an assumption undergirds biblical literalism. In contrast, a lamp is directional; it illuminates differently depending on where it is situated and how it is positioned. Using this model, we can see that the biblical writers were expressing the "reality" illuminated by their own interests and dispositions; they were reflectors of the discourse and concerns of their individual communities.[8]

It is from this latter epistemological perspective that we must understand the writings which constitute our Scriptures as well as the doctrinal and creedal statements which fill church history. What is given in the Bible we read, the creeds we recite, and the doctrines that guide our perceptions is what seemed important to the authors of these documents as they reflected the concerns— social, political, and psychological—of their communities and of themselves. To call these forms that we encounter in Christianity "social constructions" or "fictions" is not disrespectful to their intentions. It simply expresses the way in which meaning systems come into being.

The most basic fact of human experience is the recognition of our finitude and limitations. At every point we are faced with our limited ability to reflect on, and to represent, the reality we encounter. This fact is particularly evident when we attempt to speak of what is Holy and Absolute. Fictional representation through symbol and metaphor is the only means whereby we can describe that which exceeds human comprehension. Myth enables us to structure insights that will allow us to follow our quest for holistic explanations of the cosmos and to understand the meaning of our personal existence in all its ramifications. It is from this perspective that I say Christianity rests on fiction and myth—there being no other form which could enable us to speak of something so encompassing in its concerns.[9]

Yet despite the abstract and metaphysical quality of some of our questions, we desire to express our religious faith in con- crete and highly visible ways. Stated differently: we are both mind and body, and we consequently apperceive reality on both levels. Thus, we use highly concrete symbols in our worship, with architectural dynamics playing a not insignificant part in what we feel and experience. The smell and taste of wine and bread, the visual ambience created by stained-glass windows, the costuming of priests and ministers—all these appeals to our senses contribute to our impression that we are not in the profane world of everyday life. We are inextricably both flesh and spirit. Worship appeals in a highly integrated way to both these two modes of perception and experience. The temptation, however, is to reify: to make these symbols holy as if they were identical with the reality to which they point—when, in fact, they are the products of creative insight. To reify is to engage in idolatry. Protestants and Catholics alike have forgotten the warnings explicit within the Old Testament. And that is the pathology of some forms of Christian faith and practice: individuals mistake their own creations, and those of the historic church, for the Mystery itself. Orthodoxy, fundamentalism, and some expressions of evangelicalism have been especially susceptible to this perversion of Christianity.

VESSELS OF THE HOLY

The theological confusions of many Christians at the present moment may in a strange way serve as a deterrent to idolatry. The lack of certitude about the nature of God may actually represent a healthy respect for the dangers of substituting human forms for Holy Substance. In fact, to argue that all religious forms are social fictions is to be faithful to the ancient Jewish custom of refusing to utter the name of God, as well as to the modern insight that the human elaboration of reality is as much a statement about one's personal interests as it is a statement about the nature of reality itself. I am not arguing for solipsism—the theory that the self can be aware of nothing but its own experiences and that nothing exists or is real but the self—but I am suggesting that what we call reality within the religious sphere is a product of the dialectic between the individual with handheld lamp and the truth that lies beyond the full reach of the beam's illumination. Hence, our attempts to describe this reality are always partial and appropriately identified as social constructions.

But for the theologically troubled Christian who begins to identify Christianity as resting on fictive forms, the temptation is to dismiss the forms of the church (including both liturgy and doctrine) as being *misrepresentations* of the truth. This tendency rests on the mistaken idea that one could possibly have a nonfictional representation of Ultimate Reality. Perhaps most fundamentalists and a goodly number of evangelicals believe that such a thing is so—that the Bible is a mirror rather than a lamp to reality— but I am not certain that all of these who wish to identify themselves as Christians must agree.

Ironically, many highly sophisticated individuals who forsake Christianity do so on grounds that have a close affinity to the nonrelativistic stance of evangelicals. Which is to say, they reject Christianity because the forms are perceived to be socially constructed fictions, though they are aware that absolute conceptualizations of the Ultimate Mystery are impossible.

I see no reason why Christians cannot recite the creeds, participate in the sacrament of the Eucharist, and enjoy the rich symbolic structure of the church without feeling that they are somehow being hypocritical if they do not *literally* believe what they are affirming. Not to do so is to be imprisoned within a pre-Enlightenment world view. The power of the church's forms is not that they are identical with the Divine. Their purpose is to be vessels of the Holy, vehicles that point beyond themselves to the Ultimate Reality which imbues these fictional representations with power. To recite the creeds and to read the Scriptures as part of one's worship is to acknowledge that one stands in a history in which others have struggled to articulate the nature of the Ultimate and the appropriate response to be made to it.

THE SYMBOLIC FORM OF JESUS

It is from the perspective outlined above that I understand "the way to God as being through Christ." The Christ of the New Testament is that symbolic form presented to us by the Christian community of the first several centuries and the form through which they understood their relatedness to God. We continue to use this symbolic form to talk to each other about the meaning of life, death, and suffering. The symbolic representation of Jesus in the New Testament is not identical with the man who lived in the first century and was called Jesus. Yet this form symbolized in the eucharistic feast is imbued with the meaning that Jesus mediated to those early Christians who quested after a fuller experience of their Creator. The social construction those individuals created was not without relation to the man who healed and taught and fed the multitudes, but his life was interpreted from the consciousness (and interests) of those who sought meaning for their own lives.

The symbolic form of Jesus changes expression as Christians of each new generation seek to understand the meaning of life in their historical period (even though the reference point is always that image presented in the New Testament documents). The theologians of the fifth, twelfth, nineteenth, and twentieth centuries are many times removed from the Jesus of history. They interact not with the Jesus of Nazareth but with the symbolic representations of that man as pictured in the New Testament documents and the history of theological reflection, that inevitable lens through which these documents are read.

This is not to say, however, that today's theologian writes without the benefit of the Spirit. The power of Christ in our time correlates precisely with the degree to which we are able to participate in the symbolic representations of which we are heirs and to experience therein the substance that lies behind the forms.

The possibility exists that there is nothing present within the forms. It is on this point that the man or woman of faith is distinguished from the one who is agnostic to the claim of an Ultimate Reality. The error of too many individuals experiencing a crisis of faith is their assumption that in identifying the forms as fictive they have committed themselves to an agnostic position. There is a difference between the Substance (God) and its representational forms. We are condemned to social fictions—at least on the level of human expressions or representations of the Holy. The mystery of the Christian experience, however, is that there is a Reality that stands both within and beyond our humanly created symbols.

TOWARD A MORE MATURE THEOLOGY

Many liberal Christians today may be in the same position as those romantics of the eighteenth and nineteenth centuries who, having given up the God of the neoclassicists, returned to the church for solace and spiritual renewal. For these individuals, truth was not identical with the symbols of the church, but these symbolic representations provided the avenue for experiencing the Ultimate. In quite a literal sense, the church was for them the repository of truth—though in a much different way than for many of their contemporaries.

And we, I suspect, are in a similar situation today: many liberal Christians may superficially resemble their evangelical brothers and sisters. They may say the same words and participate in the same eucharistic feast. Yet they mean something quite different when they recite the creeds or take communion. For them, the Reality is not identical with the forms—the forms are fictive, the biblical accounts are social constructions—and yet tradition has proven these forms to be alive with meaning and, consequently, an avenue to the Holy. Therefore, the liberal or radical Christian may be as devoted to the church, to Christ, to the importance of worship, as the evangelical who takes a more literal view of the symbols that empower the church.

Finally, to those who are experiencing a crisis of faith, contemplating for reasons of integrity their abstention from worship and the life of the church, I would argue that God can neither be experienced in the abstract nor conceptualized intellectually without tapping the fictive power of the imagination. The Christian church is a human community, and though its forms are social constructions, the witness is that there is One who stands beyond final representation who undergirds these social fictions. To doubt radically the validity of the symbolic representations of the Christian faith may be the first step toward embracing a more mature theology that does not, in idolatrous fashion, confuse God with the manifold expressions of God.

NOTES

1. See Dean Kelley, *Why Conservative Churches Are Growing: A Study in Sociology of Religion* (New York: Harper & Row, 1972).
2. See Thomas McFaul, " 'Strictness' and Church Membership," *The Christian Century*, March 13, 1974, pp. 281–284.
3. I do not mean to imply that there is not an intellectual rationale to support the orthodox and evangelical positions. See, for example, Edward John Carnell,

The Case for Orthodox Theology (Philadelphia: Westminster Press, 1959).

4. See Peter L. Berger, *The Precarious Vision: A Sociologist Looks at Social Fictions and Christian Faith* (Garden City, N.Y.: Doubleday, 1961).

5. On Jesus as a symbolic form, see H. Richard Niebuhr, *The Responsible Self: An Essay in Christian Moral Philosophy*, with intro. by James M. Gustafson (New York: Harper & Row, 1963), pp. 154–159.

6. See H. Richard Niebuhr's excellent discussion of this and related points in *The Meaning of Revelation* (New York: Macmillan, 1941), esp. p. 47 ff.

7. See Peter L. Berger and Thomas Luckmann, *The Social Construction of Reality: A Treatise in the Sociology of Knowledge* (Garden City, N.Y.: Doubleday, 1966), pp. 88–92.

8. See Schutz's discussion of the selectivity of perception in Alfred Schutz, *The Phenomenology of the Social World*, trans. George Walsh and Frederick Lehnert, with intro. by George Walsh (Evanston, Ill.: Northwestern University Press, 1967), p. 50 ff.

9. Robert Bellah, in *Beyond Belief: Essays on Religion in a Post-Traditional World* (New York: Harper & Row, 1970), p. 203, quotes the poet Wallace Stevens: "The final belief is to believe in a fiction, which you know to be a fiction, there being nothing else. The exquisite truth is to know that it is a fiction and that you believe in it willingly."

Faith as Troubled Commitment

3

THERE ARE two famous stories that bear retelling in illustration of the argument made in the preceding chapter. One is the story of the "analogy of the cave," which appears in book seven of Plato's *Republic*.[1] The other is the parable of the Grand Inquisitor in Dostoevsky's classic novel, *The Brothers Karamazov*.[2] Although these stories were written many centuries apart, I believe both are critiques of idolatry. They both hold out a vision of a reality that exceeds human form and conceptualization.

THE ANALOGY OF THE CAVE

The situation Plato poses is that of a group of prisoners who dwell in a cave where they are chained in such a fashion that they can only cast their gaze toward the imposing wall of the cave. On the wall of the cave they regularly witness figures that dance and move. The prisoners accept these figures as real. What they do not realize is that the figures are mere shadows created by objects made of wood and stone, held up from behind a low wall situated between the prisoners and a bright fire burning high in the back of the cave.

Before continuing with Plato's story, it might be argued, by way of drawing a parallel to the topic of the previous chapter, that many conservative Christians have contented themselves with making shadows into reality. Which is to say, they have taken the writings of Scripture to be identical with the reality of God—whereas in actuality, the Bible is a collection of men's "reflections" about God, reflections that are a mere shadow of Ultimate Reality. To make a shadow into a hard reality is to fail to understand the parallel between symbols and shadows. Though shadows tell us something about the reality that gives them form, they still are reflections of (or about) something more concrete.

Plato continues his story: one day the chains are removed from the neck of a single prisoner in the cave and he is able to look around. Suddenly he becomes aware that the shadows he has taken to be reality are actually created by wood and stone figures held up from behind a wall and that the flickering fire is what makes these figures dance against the wall of the cave. A new reality is opened to the prisoner.

It seems to me that a new reality has been opened to many liberal Christians for whom the function of language and the role of symbols has been more clearly understood. Through education and scholarship they have come to realize more fully the origin of the shadows that constitute the tradition, beliefs, and worship practices of the church. The shadows are not to be discounted as being without basis; rather, they are to be appreciated and enjoyed and celebrated as the projections of those who have stood in the "light."

Plato concludes his story by describing how one day the chains are removed from the prisoner's legs so that he is able to venture toward a new source of light—the passageway to the entrance of the cave. He begins the rough ascent to the source of the diffuse light that attracts him. Upon reaching the mouth of the cave, he is blinded by the sunlight, as he had been blinded earlier by the fire light when first his chains were removed. He gropes his way out into the sunlit surface of the earth, and for the first time, he sees the wonder beyond the cave.

It seems to me that liberal Christians are those who rightly maintain that, however profound the insights they might have into the nature of religion and reality, their pronouncements from *within* the cave are *not* identical with that which exists beyond perceptions within this world. Thus, whatever theological systems the liberal Christian may create or ascribe to, he or she wisely qualifies them as "human" systems and does not confuse them with the structure of Ultimate Reality.

THE GRAND INQUISITOR

In *The Brothers Karamazov,* Ivan, the oldest brother, tells Aloysha, the youngest brother—who is thinking of entering the priesthood—a story set in sixteenth century Spain at the most terrible time of the Inquisition. It is a story that, in Plato's terms, asks whether people really want to have their chains removed: do they not prefer to be fettered because of the security that easily apprehended shadows provide? I retell the story, in spite of its familiarity, because it helps to explain why not everyone is clamoring to get on the liberal bandwagon.

In Ivan's imaginary story, Jesus himself makes an appearance in the town of Seville. He comes silently, unobtrusively, healing the sick and doing good to those around him. Although he does not announce who he is, people seem to recognize him. A crowd follows him. On the day on which Ivan's story centers, a young girl is brought to Jesus in a casket. He touches her and brings her back to life. The cardinal, the Grand Inquisitor, watches from a distance, and when he sees the girl resurrected from the dead, he sends his guards to arrest Jesus. The crowd parts to make way for the guards, who seize Jesus and take him to the prison in the ancient palace. When the people see who it is that is arresting Jesus, they bow to the old Inquisitor—who stands tall and erect, a man in his nineties, with a withered face and sunken eyes that still contain a gleam of light—and he in turn blesses the people in silence.

That night, in pitch darkness, the iron door of the prison opens and the Grand Inquisitor enters. He carries in his hand a light, which he silently places on the table opposite his prisoner. Then he speaks: "Is it Thou? Thou?" But receiving no answer, he sighs: "What canst Thou say? . . . Thou hast no right to add anything to what Thou hadst said of old." He is not stopped, however, by Jesus' silence. He accusingly says to his prisoner: "Thou hast come to hinder us." And he informs Jesus that the next day he will burn him at the stake. He also tells his prisoner that the very people who today kissed his feet will tomorrow rush to heap embers on the fire that will consume him.

At this point in Ivan's story, Aloysha interrupts, asking if the old man was mistaken about who his prisoner was. No, replies

Ivan. Ivan goes on to tell Aloysha of the dialogue which followed between Jesus and the Grand Inquisitor. The Grand Inquisitor tells Jesus that the people do not want freedom—which is what Jesus offered them. Instead they want bread—the authority supplied by the priestly class. Only a few, the heretics whom the Grand Inquisitor burns daily, prefer freedom. But in contrast to these few heretics who desire freedom, the old man tells his prisoner, there are ten thousand who prefer the security of the existing structure.

> So long as man remains free he survives for nothing so incessantly and so painfully as to find someone to worship. But man seeks to worship what is established beyond dispute, so that all men would agree at once to worship it.[3]

The Grand Inquisitor rehearses Jesus' earthly temptations and acknowledges that in each case his prisoner elected freedom over the security born of miracle. But accusingly, in the same breath, he asserts that *men* prefer security to freedom. To his prisoner the Grand Inquisitor declares:

> We [the priestly class] have corrected Thy work and have founded it upon *miracle, mystery* and *authority*. And men rejoiced that they were again led like sheep, and that the terrible gift [freedom] that had brought them such suffering was, at last, lifted from their hearts.[4] (emphasis added)

The Grand Inquisitor confronts his prisoner with the fact that Jesus misjudged what men wanted when he came to earth the first time. What does mankind seek? In answer, he asserts: "someone to worship, someone to keep his conscience, and some means of uniting all in one unanimous and harmonious ant-heap, for the craving for universal unity is the third and last anguish of man."[5] Who then loves humanity more? The Grand Inquisitor asserts that he and his fellow priests do. The only unhappy ones, in fact, are the priests who know the secret of the mystery: that there is no life after the grave. But would a lover of humanity broadcast such knowledge?

Ivan ends his story by saying that when the Grand Inquisitor had finished speaking, he waited for a reply from his prisoner. The old man yearned for a response, even a rebuke, but none came. Instead, the prisoner approached the old man and softly kissed him on his bloodless, aged lips. The old man shuddered, says Ivan, and then stood, opened the door of the cell, and said, "Go, and come no more." He led his prisoner out into the dark alleys of the town where the prisoner disappeared, never to return again.

The liberal Christian is in many ways less secure than most fundamentalists and conservative evangelicals. Truth is more ambiguous, requires greater deliberation and qualification. The liberal Christian does not have a four-step plan for achieving salvation.[6] Faith is viewed as a never-ending process. In short, *miracle, mystery,* and *authority* play a much stronger role for many conservative Christians than for most liberals. Liberal Christians are more likely to seek for the miraculous in a broken relationship that has been healed than in an act where the laws of nature are defiled. Liberal Christians may embrace the mystery of Ultimate Truth, but they seldom seek the mystery of oracles and private revelations. And authority is granted to that One who slays all finite images of the Absolute, as opposed to the authority which can be affixed to a human personality.

RADICAL MONOTHEISM

The insight of central importance, I believe, is that whereas the symbolic forms of the church may be partial and limited, conditioned by the particular socio-historical circumstances in which they arose, and thus bear all the marks of the process of the human imputation of meaning, they nevertheless exist as forms that potentially mediate the unconditioned. In other words, they themselves are conditioned and of human origin, but the reality they portend is not. Thus, while the symbolic forms of the church may mediate the Truth, they are *not* identical with the Truth. This is a simple distinction, but one which is important for it allows Christians to acknowledge religious forms as social constructions—legitimating social-psychological analysis of them—and at the same time remain deeply committed to the possibility of there being a reality that these forms potentially mediate.

As noted in chapter 2, the most profound elements of Judaism have always maintained that to describe God through human forms is idolatry. The prophetic tradition, as well as the more general heritage of radical monotheism,[7] has been suspect of any human attempt to define the nature of God. God is that One who exceeds comprehension, whose only name is "I Am." Sacrament and creed are mere links bridging the gap between God and man; they are not to be taken as ends in themselves. Such an elevated view of God is difficult to sustain, for it does not offer material support. But maintain it we must.

Many of us presently find ourselves being stripped of our assurances: about the church, the nature and reality of God, and the path to faith. The concrete God of childhood has been revealed to be a fatherly projection; the Bible stories we may have learned have since assumed the status of epic and legend; the charisma of priests and ministers who once served our call for authority has been discovered to derive from human sanction. But is it not possible that the present *Kairos*[8] in which our limiting notions of God are being shattered is not for ill, but is in continuity with the prophetic demand to cast off idolatry? I believe that we should not bemoan the passing of the "age of belief." The starkness of the alternatives before us—nihilism or a radical monotheism that offers little material support—is the precondition for faith in a God who allows no other gods before him. Neither bibliolatry nor sacerdotalism is viable. In their place stands our freedom: a freedom that may lead us into prayer and worship because there, and no place else, we find a porthole to the realm of the Holy.

TROUBLED COMMITMENT

The option I find viable for myself is one that might be identified as "troubled commitment": to the church and to the forms that have served her for nearly two millennia. This is the way of commitment beyond belief, faith without an objectifying assurance. Troubled commitment is a stage beyond the revelry of demythologization. It stands on the recognition that, through participation in the symbolic forms of the church, self-transcendence is possible; that the sacraments of the church, even the creeds, are social constructions that historically have provided a means for glimpsing the eternal verities which order the universe. The man who worships with troubled commitment finds in the enigmas of the church's central symbols (and their accompanying stories) that poetic structure which is transparent to the most Ultimate of realities.

For all its hypocrisy, the church is a worthy object of troubled commitment because in modern society it stands as a nearly solitary example of moral community—or at least of a symbolic gesture towards it. The church provides a vocabulary for talking about moral obligation, forgiveness, and reconciliation between persons and among communities. The church is in possession of a fund of experiences, paradigms, and symbols that enable individuals to reflect on the nature of the good life, the good society, and one's responsibility for achieving these within a community of like-minded individuals. Furthermore, the church has evolved forms that enable the community to deal with moral transgression and failures of human hope.

The fact that these symbolic forms are of human creation may disillusion some. Some may find them lacking in intrinsic worth—and indeed they are. Because the sacraments of the church, the creeds that elaborate a basis for communal unity, are not of value except for the intentionality one grants to them. They are vessels and instruments through which one may experience and partake of the Ultimate Reality, but they are not ultimate in themselves. If a form becomes established as an end in itself, it warrants displacement. The tradition of radical monotheism avers that the only reality is that Spirit which stands behind, and enlivens, the symbolic forms which have evolved within the human community.

COMPETING PATHS

Christmas, Easter—they portend a reality in which men and women have found a gateway to Truth. Other traditions are available. But it makes little sense to imagine that one can feed simultaneously from all the manifold fountains of spiritual existence. Epistemological relativism may appear to be an invitation to worship at every shrine the world offers. But such eclecticism only produces a discordant spirit. Whatever Ultimate Unity there may be beyond the realm of sentient beings, each religious tradition lays claim to its own symbolic integration and stylistic integrity. In the religious life, depth is almost always to be preferred to breadth. Only a few great spirits can successfully manage a syncretism of forms, realizing the depth of each.

Of course an individual may elect to make the religious pilgrimage on his or her own without the benefit of those evolved symbols that mark the way of other seekers after Truth. One may eschew corporate commitments and deny the value of mere "myths" of human origin and ultimate meaning. Surely the social sciences provide for many the assurance of a system that offers more secure boundaries than those of radical monotheism. Within such a system, technical vocabulary is substituted for poetic imagery, ritual is dismissed as outmoded primitivism, and the material world provides the sole sphere for flights of imagination. To follow such a course is to be decidedly modern. But does modernity necessarily supply the noblest standard for human virtue and the quest for meaning?

Social science spins its own dogmas. But marathon therapy weekends will never replace monastic retreats. Psychiatrists will not displace priests. I believe that description and prescription differ; that the material world and the world of ultimate meanings and values warrant different rhetorics and different symbolic communities. In my view, the social-scientific and the theological provinces of discourse do not conflict, and, indeed, they may even interpenetrate. Why? Because they deal with different facets of man's being and have their separate ways of understanding these different aspects.[9]

Unlike abstract formulations, myth and fiction have a capacity for holistic explanation. Poetic forms deal not with the sphere of mechanism and design, but with purpose, emotion, and value. The nativity and the resurrection narratives illumine a different reality than stimulus-response equations. Furthermore, the one is meant to be told and retold, interpreted and reinterpreted, because as symbolic form it admits to multivalent layers of meaning. The value of the other is its precision of explanation or prediction. They both, however, have their place. But whereas the body is nurtured by empirical substance, the spirit is enlivened by that flame which illumines images of human aspiration for wholeness and self-transcendence.

UNITY IN WORSHIP

What dogmatists of both liberal and conservative persuasions often fail to realize is that religious stories may fulfill their function of stimulating moral and metaphysical imagination on a literal as well as on a symbolic level (which is fortunate, given the fact that not all individuals share the same mentality nor experiences). There will always be literalists in the religious community, just as there will always be those with a more symbolic inclination. Both can worship in the same community, imbibing the same stories. Likewise they can recite the same creeds and receive the same sacraments. Professors and laborers can worship together—as can liberals and conservatives—for to each the form is the same, and for each, I would assert, the Reality is identical. Only the interpretation differs. Salvation rests not in the forms, nor even in their interpretation, but in the Reality which they mediate—and one's experience of it.

NOTES

1. Plato, *The Dialogues of Plato,* vol. 1, trans. B. Jowett, with intro. by Raphael Demos (New York: Random House, 1937), pp. 773–776.
2. Fyodor Dostoevsky, *The Brothers Karamazov,* trans. Constance Garnett, rev. and ed. Ralph E. Matlaw (New York: W. W. Norton, 1976), pp. 227–245.
3. Ibid., p. 234.
4. Ibid., p. 237.
5. Ibid., p. 238.
6. I refer, of course, to the "copyrighted" *Four Spiritual Laws* of Campus Crusade for Christ.
7. See the collection of essays by H. Richard Niebuhr, *Radical Monotheism and Western Culture: With Supplementary Essays* (New York: Harper & Row, 1960).
8. See the discussion of the term *Kairos* by Paul Tillich, *The Protestant Era,* abr. ed. (Chicago: University of Chicago Press, Phoenix Books, 1957), pp. 32–51.
9. On the distinction between science and religion, see Ernst Cassirer, *An Essay on Man: An Introduction to a Philosophy of Human Culture* (New Haven, Conn.: Yale University Press, 1944), pp. 72–108, 207–221.

The Liberal Agenda

4

I BELIEVE that any attempt to reenvision the liberal agenda appropriately begins with an assumption that every individual desires some frame of reference from which he or she may view life as meaningful. Although individuals may be relatively inarticulate concerning the nature and structure of this framework, it is their framework of meaning, nevertheless, which gives them a reason to awake in the morning and to pursue a round of activities. As a framework, it includes a scheme of values. It also contains some statement regarding the significance of one's own life. And it may include views on such issues as the finality of death. It is the desire for a framework of values and meaning which defines, in my view, the essential humanity of man and distinguishes human beings from the rest of the animal kingdom.

One of the central facts of contemporary existence is the diversity of meaning systems that individuals follow. Liberal Christianity is one framework of meaning and values. In addition to being unique as a religious framework of meaning—as opposed to a strictly secular framework, which makes no reference to things sacred, or to a transcendent reference point for evaluating the meaningfulness of human existence—liberal Christianity is distinctive insofar as it is one of several perspectives within the Christian religious framework.

In concluding this section of the book, I wish to describe some of the unique characteristics of the liberal perspective. My intent is not to give an historical account of liberalism—for there are many available[1]—but to provide a normative interpretation of what I believe to be important to a contemporary expression of liberal Christianity. In my opinion, the time is ripe for a revitalization of the liberal tradition along the lines of some of its distinctive hallmarks. I believe there can be, and should be, as much conviction, vigor, and excitement within the liberal church as there is among evangelicals, charismatics, and other branches of Christendom. Conservatives do not have an exclusive hold on the Spirit. Indeed, the liberal Christians' openness to the world places them in a position of vital importance in contemporary society.

DEFINING LIBERAL CHRISTIANITY

Liberal Christians differ from their more conservative counterparts at a number of points, but let me begin with their *view towards culture.* Rather than perceiving culture, particularly science and the arts, as a potential threat to religious faith, liberal Christians characteristically have sought to understand their faith with reference to their experience within contemporary culture. Liberal Christians have understood that Christianity must evolve and adapt itself—or at least its expression—from age to age. They have believed that the application of the gospel must be reinterpreted from each new cultural context.[2] Although there may be a core essence to Christianity, liberal Christians view accommodation to culture as necessary and positive, if what one means by "accommodation" is that they should seek to understand God and their moral responsibility in terms of the best available scientific knowledge and social analysis (see chapter 8).

The Arts and Education

Liberal Christians look upon the arts as important expressions of the problems and tensions of their culture. Liberal Christians also recognize the invaluable moral critiques found in many artistic expressions. Whereas film, theatre, and dance may be shunned by many conservative Christians, liberal Christians look to these artistic productions as important occasions for not only self-reflection, but also a potential uplifting and enlivening of the human spirit. Liberal Christians have long recognized that things ultimate and real can be portrayed through a variety of mediums. Thus, an evening spent reading a novel, viewing a theatrical production, or seeing a movie may be as illuminating as a comparable period of time spent reading the Bible. Liberal Christians believe that revelations may come in many forms.

Liberals have long been champions of education. They find that nothing is to be feared in knowledge. To discover the relativity of cultures is not a new insight so much as it is a foundation stone on which liberalism rests. Liberal clergy have usually been highly educated. The task implicit in sermon preparation by liberal clergy has been to blend creatively the "old gospel" with the personal, social, and political problems felt by those in the pew. As a result, psychological, sociological, and philosophical insights often have found their way into the text of sermons given by the liberal clergy. Book discussion groups have been at least as common in liberal churches as Bible study groups and prayer meetings.

The danger in liberalism is that the Christian message may become a mirror reflection of the spirit of the age. This is an ever-present problem for liberal Christians to confront. On the other hand, liberals have protested that one cannot possibly critique culture without understanding it; hence, the importance of witnessing the cultural production of the arts and sciences. Nevertheless, it is in losing the tension between Christ and culture that liberal Christianity has most frequently lost its soul. This is a problem that repeatedly needs to be addressed (and this is the focus of parts III and IV of this book).

Morality

Liberal Christians have always placed considerable emphasis upon the moral witness of their faith. Rooted in the Social Gospel Movement of the last several decades of the nineteenth century and the first three decades of the twentieth century,[3] liberal Christianity has always sought to apply its Gospel to the social betterment of the human community. Political rallies and social action committee meetings have often taken the place of more traditionally pious activities. In its earlier period, liberalism was married to the spirit of socialism. As political winds changed, so did the social ethic of liberal Christianity. Under the pressure of the Neo-orthodox Movement, many liberals were forced into a greater acknowledgment of the reality of sin and of the necessity of a newfound political realism. Whatever the ideology, however, liberal Christians have always found themselves in the streets, politicking city councils, writing letters to congressmen, and busying themselves with social welfare concerns. Their approach stands in contrast to that of many conservative Christians who have sought to change the world by changing hearts (through conversion).

Although Scripture and tradition are important, the basepoint of liberal morality has been reason. This emphasis, of course, has coincided nicely with the commitment of liberal Christians to education. In contrast to the scriptural "proof-texting" of many conservative Christians, liberals have often appealed to the broader principles of justice and love as explicated in the Bible. Reason has always been the mediating force in applying these biblical insights to particular situations. Not infrequently liberals have endorsed a contextual or situational ethic. They have been relatively inhospitable, on the other hand, to moral legalisms. Always reason is to be used in weighing the authority of Scripture and tradition.

In evaluating social and cultural issues, liberal Christians have often turned to the social sciences for their interpretative categories. In fact, the Social Gospel Movement directly paralleled what was known at the turn of the century as "Christian sociology." An inordinately large number of early American sociologists were former clergy or came out of families dominated by clergy. Presently, the link between liberal Christianity and the social sciences continues to be expressed as many a former priest or minister finds his or her vocation as a clinical psychologist or social worker.

Another identifying mark of the moral commitment of liberal Christians is that they have characteristically given at least as much attention to social morality as personal morality. Matters of sexual practice and personal vice have been of interest to liberal Christians, but programmatic emphases have more typically been related to issues of war, poverty, racial discrimination, employment practices, and so forth. Systemic and social-structural problems have been understood to be at the root of much of the suffering and misery in the world. For this reason, the prophets of the Old Testament have often been appealed to as frequently as the teachings of Jesus.

Scripture

Liberal Christians differ from conservative Christians in that they generally approach Scripture nondogmatically. Liberal biblical scholars tend to apply historical, sociological, and even psychological tools and insights to their interpretations of Scripture. The hermeneutical principle often applied is that everything—Scripture included—is written within a cultural context. Therefore, to understand the meaning of a document, one must understand how and why it was written. One must also understand the world view of the writer. For example, one of the most famous biblical scholars, Rudolf Bultmann, believed that the New Testament was written from the perspective of a prescientific cosmology of a three-tiered universe (with heaven above, hell or the underworld below, and the earth, on which men and women dwell, as a mediating structure between the two). His task of demythologization was an effort to get at the kerygma (message) which lay behind this first century world view.[4]

When the Scriptures are understood as human documents, they then are susceptible to all the canons of modern historical and literary analysis. To the liberal theologian, there is a considerable difference between viewing the Bible primarily through the eyes of faith and being equally open to a cultural and historical perspective. Historically, the resurrection of Jesus and the virgin birth are at best ambiguous as concrete occurrences. From the perspective of faith, however, they may have quite a different significance. But one should never conclude that the Scriptures are unimportant for the liberal Christian. Quite the contrary, they are central to the Christian faith. The fact that more attention is given to them as symbolic documents than as historical documents does not distort their importance.

After all, liberal Christianity (as well as fundamentalist Christianity) is based upon a message whose inspiration is taken from the life and teachings of Jesus. Whatever accommodations are to be made in applying Christianity to the contemporary setting, the liberal Christian is nevertheless compelled to go back to the rather radical teachings of Jesus concerning the kingdom. Any compromises to be made with the Sermon on the Mount, for example, are self-consciously made by understanding the setting in which Jesus was teaching and living. Likewise, any alterations of Paul's teachings on women are made, again, from the basis of an interpretation of Paul's social setting. Liberal Christians, by their very approach to Scripture, are spared the agony experienced by many conservatives who are forced, when they disagree with some biblical dictum on the grounds of social conscience, to go through what has been aptly described as a sort of "hermeneutical ventriloquism."[5]

God

A basic distinction to be drawn between liberal and conservative Christians concerns the issue of God's self-declaration to man. Most conservative Christians begin with the assumption that man exists as the creation of God, a supernatural being who is personal and therefore interested in communicating with his creation. Following on this assumption, conservative Christians postulate that God has revealed himself in time and space at a number of historical junctures, the most important being his decision to give earthly form to his son, Jesus. Jesus, then, is viewed as God's clearest self-declaration of who he is. Furthermore, conservative Christians postulate that God safeguarded his self-declaration by inspiring the writers of the Bible, giving them the very words to say (or, some would argue, only the thoughts were given—while others more liberal, but still within the conservative camp, would argue that God gave official sanction to what was penned by the biblical writers).[6]

Liberal Christians, on the other hand, tend to see the above progression as much too anthropomorphic. Even the father-son imagery seems like a projection. Rather than starting with God, postulating divine initiative, many liberal Christians begin with the human predicament and emphasize *man's search* for God. According to this approach, from the standpoint of a functional definition, God is synonymous with the search for human wholeness, for confidence in the ultimate meaningfulness of human existence. Paul Tillich's definition of faith as the *state* of Ultimate Concern is representative of the liberal perspective because the emphasis is placed upon man's search for God.[7]

Tillich's definition of God, too, is representative of the liberal position. God is the "God above God"—meaning that man's finite limitations forever leave man short of defining in any absolute way who God is.[8] Nevertheless, to the extent that one dares to venture a definition, it is an expansive one: God is the very "Ground of Being"; God is "Being-Itself."[9] These definitions are nonreductive. If liberals have a central objection to the view many conservative Christians pose of God, it is that the conservative view reduces God to understandable, human terms—or human projections. Tillich's view of God as the "Ground of Being" is in reaction to that first century cosmological perspective which put God up in the sky, sitting on a throne, looking down on his creation.

Liberal Christians have viewed God in a much more immanentistic fashion. God is within creation. He is the lifeforce. He is at the center of all change, all innovation, all creativity. He is the source of life and is experienced in those profound moments of joy, communion, celebration. God is the "Thou" of the I-Thou encounter. He is the Ground of Being. God is present in all those activities which unite people rather than divide them, which call upon persons to transcend self-interest through brotherhood and sisterhood. God is personal as we discover our own humanity and act in his name to realize community: that state in which we relate to others as "ends" and not "means" to self-centered purposes.

The finer expressions about God in the liberal tradition have not, however, made God totally immanent.[10] While many liberal Christians may have moved toward a healthy mysticism in both their experience and their speech about God, they have maintained the tension between God as transcendent and God as immanent. In other words, they have recognized, above all, that it is idolatrous to reduce God to human standards. He is present within his creation, he is the source of all meaning, he is at the center of all ethical structures, and yet he stands above and outside that which is purely human as the judge of all human projects. He is the "I am" of the Old Testament. He is one to both fear and worship.

SYMBOLIC REALISM

Sociologist Robert Bellah has identified an important distinction between two types of "realism" that separate conservatives from liberals.[11] Conservatives tend to be "historical realists" to the extent that they believe the truth of Christianity is found in the historical acts witnessed to in the New Testament—such as literal miracles, a literal bodily resurrection, and so forth. Historical realists are interested in understanding history "as it was." They take a nonmetaphorical and nonfigurative approach to interpreting Scripture. Reality is taken to reside in the events of history rather than in the interpretive nexus that exists between subject (interpreter) and object (actual event). Such an approach moves one toward equating faith with acceptance of a set of doctrinal propositions about the "historical record" of the Bible. Hence, one is "saved" if one believes that the Bible is the inspired word of God, that Jesus is the literal son of God sent down to earth to atone for mankind's sins, that he died on the cross and three days later was miraculously raised from the dead, and that he presently lives with God, sitting at his right hand.

The liberal "symbolic realists," in contrast, emphasize that "meaning" is always a product of the interaction between subject and object. Meaning is *granted* to events—it is not considered inherent in them. According to this view, the Scriptures contain the record of men's and women's reflections regarding the *meaning* which Christ had *for them*. It is not primarily an historical account. The resurrection, the miracles, the virgin birth are valued as symbols that point beyond the historical event to a larger and more ultimate truth. But the truth does not lie in the symbols (as historical events). Symbols are irreducible. They are not identical with actual events, although they may derive from them. To take symbols literally is to engage in idolatry. Symbolic realists have given up hope of discovering what "really happened"; indeed, most of them are not even convinced that such knowledge would make much difference.

The symbols that surround the life of Christ—parables, stories, sayings, etc.—are understood by liberal Christians to be vitally important. It is through the symbol of Christ (which is a complex symbol, indeed) that men and women may come to know God. The symbolic form of Christ, as presented in the Gospel accounts, however, points beyond any purely historical events to a transcendent Truth or Reality (which we symbolize as God)—this is the hope and faith of liberal Christians.

Symbols, then, are not endpoints; they are mediators which exist between the worshipping Christian and the God who orders and sustains all reality. To call Christ a symbolic form is not iconoclastic, it is simply a recognition that something occurred— the imputing of meaning—in the transition for the biblical writers from their perception of Jesus, the man, to Christ, the Son of God, the hope for all eternity.

AN EMPIRICAL AND CONFESSIONAL AFFIRMATION

Liberal Christians value reason, particularly as applied to moral reflection, but few liberals believe that a purely rational system can be built to explain that Ultimate Reality identified as God. Hence, strictly rational deductions concerning God are often shunned by liberals, as are rational "proofs" for the existence of God. Liberal Christians tend to be much more "confessional" and "empirical" in their approach. They elect to reason about what they perceive to be their experience of God. There is no Christian God per se, only Christians' reflections about God.[12] And what is it that Christians reflect about? Surely it is their experience—as individuals, as a corporate group—in the quest for what is right and true and beautiful.

Liberal Christians are often weary of "doctrines" of inspiration and revelation and incarnation. Surely God has revealed and could reveal himself. But liberal Christians are impressed by the limitations of perception, the role of intentionality in granting meaning, the conditionedness of time and place, and the confines of language adequate to "capture" God.

Recognition by liberal Christians of the mythological character of many of the biblical accounts, attention to the social conditionedness of the thought patterns of the biblical writers, and repudiation of the "factual content" (as opposed to symbolic character) of the church's historic creeds and doctrines, however, opened the way to totally humanizing the Christian faith. This is what orthodox Christians had always thought about liberals— that they were merely disguised humanists.[13] Indeed, emerging in the 1960s were a spate of theologians announcing the "death of God."[14] Many of these persons made their way to this position from the neo-orthodox camp, but not a few came from the ranks of liberalism. The common meeting point was a collapsed metaphysic. Either God had become so transcendent that he evaporated like a vapor into the sky, or else he was was so immanent that it was difficult to distinguish him from nature.

Preceding the announcements in *Time* magazine that God was dead, then Bishop John A. T. Robinson wrote a seemingly innocuous book entitled *Honest to God*.[15] It turned out, however, that the book was not so innocuous. Although Robinson, by his own admission, was doing little more than popularizing Paul Tillich, Rudolf Bultmann, Joseph Fletcher, and others, the book exploded on the market like a bombshell. Obviously the cultural conditions were such that the public was ripe to hear the bishop's confession.[16]

The only difficulty in the public response to *Honest to God*— and, I would argue, in the faddish proclamation of the death of God—was that people were much too literalistic. They refused to understand the subtlety of analysis *and* the power of experience of symbolic forms. The neo-orthodox had forgotten immanence, the counterpart to the transcendence of God, and the liberals in their passion to make God "relevant" had forgotten his transcendence. Theologians such as H. Richard Niebuhr had spoken years earlier with rightful dismay concerning those who dismissed Christ as "only a symbol."[17]

RECOVERING LIBERALISM

It is my opinion that what is needed in the churches today is a wide-scale recovery of the liberal spirit. Paul Tillich, H. Richard Niebuhr, Rudolf Bultmann, and others left a heritage that fell into reductionistic hands before it could appropriately be assimilated on a popular level. I believe that it is perhaps time to go back and reread *Honest to God*. There are insights contained there, regarding the state of theology in the fifties and early sixties, that warrant rethinking. Tillich was not an immanentalist. Bultmann did not think the Bible was bunk. Joseph Fletcher was not a "do your own thing" narcissist.[18]

The alternatives to liberalism are limited. About evangelicalism I have already intimated a great deal. Liberation theology is another vital expression of Christianity.[19] But however well placed liberation theology is in its Latin America setting, it is questionable whether it is equally applicable to the North American and European contexts. Indeed, in terms of a return to liberalism, I doubt if we have yet outgrown the love-power-justice dialectic announced by both Paul Tillich and Reinhold Niebuhr.[20] Cold war politics, tax initiatives that shrink the number of dollars available for health, education, libraries, and other essential services—these do not call out for a Marxist paradigm so much as a classical liberal position on distributive justice. And the ethical maxim of love can be left for the ample personal opportunities under the present social conditions for ministering to isolated individuals who are casualties of the system.

My suggestion, then, is that our social situation is ripe for a rebirth of Christian liberalism. But the ethical perspective of liberalism is only one reason for the return. Even more persuasive, in my view, is the fact that in the last decade Christendom has become polarized. With a burgeoning population of evangelicals on one side and radical secularists on the other, the *mediating position*—I would say, the *temperate alternative*—of liberalism is being lost. Many young people today are unaware that there even is an option to the left of evangelicalism. And for many secularists, particularly young people, the only alternative to evangelicalism— if one wants to be religious—is membership with the "Moonies" or the Hare Krishna cult.

I do not deny historical realists their place under the Christian sun. It is a legitimate option that will always have its appeal. But what of the symbolic realists? Clearly I am of the disposition to revitalize liberalism. In my view, liberalism is the most viable mode for reasserting the value of the Christian perspective to contemporary culture.

NOTES

1. See, for example, Harold L. DeWolf, *The Case for Theology in Liberal Perspective* (Philadelphia: Westminister Press, 1959); also see William Hordern, *A Layman's Guide to Protestant Theology*, rev. ed. (New York: Macmillan, 1968), pp. 73–110.
2. On theology as "correlation" (or mediation between religion and culture), see Paul Tillich, *Systematic Theology*, vol. 1 (Chicago: University of Chicago Press, 1951), pp. 59–65.
3. See, for example, Walter Rauschenbusch, *Christianity and the Social Crisis* (New York: Macmillan, 1907).
4. See Rudolf Bultmann, *Theology of the New Testament*, trans. Kendrick Grobel (New York: Charles Scribner's Sons, 1951), esp. pp. 33–62.
5. Robert M. Price, "A Fundamentalist Social Gospel?" *The Christian Century*, November 28, 1979, p. 1184.
6. See, for example, Jack Rogers and Donald K. McKim, *The Authority and Interpretation of the Bible: An Historical Approach* (San Francisco: Harper & Row, 1979).
7. See Paul Tillich, *Dynamics of Faith*, ed. Ruth Nanda Anshen (New York: Harper & Row, 1957), pp. 1–29.
8. See Paul Tillich, *The Courage to Be* (New Haven, Conn.: Yale University Press, 1967), p. 182 ff.
9. See Paul Tillich, *Systematic Theology*, vol. 1 (Chicago: University of Chicago Press, 1951), pp. 238–40.
10. For an excellently balanced perspective, see John Macquarrie, *Thinking about God* (New York: Harper & Row, 1975).
11. See Robert Bellah, *Beyond Belief: Essays on Religion in a Post-Traditional World* (New York: Harper & Row, 1970), pp. 247–257.
12. See the statement of H. Richard Niebuhr, *The Responsible Self: An Essay in Christian Moral Philosophy*, with intro. by James M. Gustafson (New York: Harper & Row, 1963), p. 45.
13. See Joseph Fletcher's confessional statement of his conversion to humanism in "An Odyssey: From Theology to Humanism," *Religious Humanism* 13, no. 4 (Autumn 1979): 146–157.
14. See, for example, Gabriel Vahanian, *The Death of God: The Culture of Our Post-Christian Era* (New York: George Braziller, 1961).
15. John A. T. Robinson, *Honest to God* (Philadelphia: Westminster Press, 1963).
16. See David Lawrence Edwards, ed., *The "Honest to God" Debate; Some Reactions to the Book "Honest to God"* (Philadelphia: Westminster Press, 1963).
17. Niebuhr, *The Responsible Self*, p. 157.
18. Joseph Fletcher, *Situation Ethics, The New Morality* (Philadelphia: Westminster Press, 1966).
19. See, for example, Juan Luis Segundo, *Liberation of Theology*, trans. John Drury (Mary Knoll, N.Y.: Orbis Books, 1976); also see Gustavo Gutierrez and M. Richard Shaull, *Liberation and Change*, ed. (with intro. by) Ronald H. Stone (Atlanta: John Knox Press, 1977).
20. See, for example, Paul Tillich, *Love, Power, and Justice: Ontological Analyses and Ethical Applications* (New York: Oxford University Press, 1960); also see Reinhold Niebuhr, *Love and Justice: Selections from the Shorter Writings*, ed. D. B. Robertson (New York: Meridian Books, 1967).

CONSTRUCTING
CHRISTIAN IDENTITY

III

Components of a Christian Life-Style

5

THE TERM *life-style* means many different things. During the 1960s the word *life-style* was usually preceded by the modifier *alternative,* and the phrase was used to refer to communal living and other countercultural expressions. In the 1970s and now in the eighties, the term *life-style* has taken on an even more specific connotation referring to new patterns of intimacy—from open marriage to swinging.[1] I wish, however, to use the term in a somewhat more traditional way to refer to the values structuring the various components of one's life: work, leisure, marital relations, organizational affiliations, political involvements, and so forth.[1] Such a usage of the term is consistent with the writings on life-style of two turn-of-the-century social scientists, Max Weber and Alfred Adler.

DEFINING LIFE-STYLE

Weber believed that society is stratified according to different "status groups," which are distinguished by the life-styles of their members. For Weber, life-style functions as an ordering mechanism within society, both providing the basis for social cohesion within a group as well as a point of demarcation between groups.[3] Adler examined life-style from a more psychological perspective and argued that every individual's thoughts and actions constitute a unity—a consistent strain running through them—which may be identified as the "style" of the individual. The source of personal style is the fact that individuals structure their existence according to particular "fictional goals" that they project; these "fictions" provide both a *goal* for structuring choices and a *filter* through which the world is perceived and its meaning is interpreted.[4]

H. Richard Niebuhr is one of a number of theologians who argue for the virtue of analyzing Christianity in life-style terms. He believed that Christians should be distinguishable from members of other religious communities on the basis of their unique style of life.[5] Inspired, in part, by Niebuhr, the task of this chapter is twofold: (1) to examine some of the elements of the Christian life-style as it has been historically defined, and (2) to articulate a normative model of the life-style of the liberal Christian.[6]

It is my conviction that Christians should express a distinctive style of life, one that distinguishes them from their neighbors— or else Christianity ceases to be very compelling. If Christianity is simply a set of theological propositions whose affirmation does not alter the way we live, then we must wonder whether Christianity is saying anything at all. The pragmatic tradition has considerable validity in its emphasis upon understanding truth in terms of the consequences of a doctrine or proposition.[7]

RELIGION AND LIFE-STYLE

There are two different ways of imaging the relationship between religion and life-style. According to the first, religion is a *subsymbol.* The car one drives, the house one lives in, the job one has, all of these are subsymbols which, when taken together, comprise a "complex symbol in motion."[8] Religion, according to this model, is one potential component—or subsymbol—of life-style, along with a number of other purchasable or assumable entities.

An alternative model of the relationship of life-style to religion places religion at the very core of one's being, with religious values functioning in a determinative role, guiding the choices one makes in constituting the variety of subsymbols that comprise one's style of life. In this model, one's religious commitments become normative for the rest of one's life-style choices. Although I wish to argue that this second model is the most viable way for the Christian to look at the way religion relates to life-style, the first model more accurately characterizes much actual religious practice.

In the contemporary period, life-style choices are made increasingly on the basis of taste rather than moral or religious values.[9] From this perspective, an individual may select Christianity as part of the larger gestalt of life-style choices; thus, religion functions not in a normative role, but in an aesthetic one. Commentators on the function of religion in American society—Will Herberg being one example—have been rightly condemnatory of a religious form in which *God serves man* rather than *man serves God*.[10]

Herberg sees little tension on the part of most people between the American way of life and their religious commitments. Herberg, a Jew, finds that conception of religion incongruous with the Judeo-Christian tradition in which religion is more than a way of sociability or belonging. According to Herberg, the religious experience should be something that reaches down into the core of existence, shattering and renewing life.[11] In this model, then, one's religious commitments (and experience) should be at the very center of one's being, ordering all other choices. The pressures of contemporary culture, however, are strongly opposed to making religion anything other than an ancillary subsymbol that is part of one's larger life-style configuration.

The dominant character type in contemporary culture is therapeutic and narcissistic (see chapter 11). That is to say, individuals prize release and catharsis over commitment and conviction, self-fulfillment and self-actualization over self-denial and self-forgetfulness. Is it any wonder that those committed to realizing the classic Christian adage that "it is only in losing one's life that one finds it" are an endangered species? The principal threat to Christianity in the present age is not, as once might have been conceived, the rivalry of other religious traditions. Rather, it is the broad-scale cultural value honoring *self*-realization over corporate commitment, the positive sanction given to living without controls, which threatens the religious community—since the religious community necessarily prizes commitment and self-discipline.

It is in the void of a rather degenerate pluralism that liberal Christianity can make its claim to uniqueness. That is, Christianity's distinctive quality derives from its potential to provide identity that is rooted in ultimate values, rather than in personal taste. For all the freedom that prevails in American culture, there is also an underlying anxiety, fueled by a sense that there is nothing absolute outside the self. It is in this context—a melancholic void—that liberal Christianity's cultural uniqueness is potentially realized: but only if the church does not itself become a purely therapeutic community, prizing release over conviction and commitment, and matters of taste over a sense of the absolute claim of a radically present, yet transcendent, God.

In short, I believe it is imperative for the Christian community to lay claim to the normative model found in the New Testament picture of Jesus' life and teachings. It is only in affirming particular principles, in committing oneself to a set of persuasive images, stories, and guidelines—as well as to a community—that character and identity may be realized. To stand for nothing is to be without a "self." One may thereby live guiltlessly, for there are no proscriptions to violate. But one also lives without meaning: one's actions derive from a void that has no center.

BASEPOINTS OF THE CHRISTIAN LIFE

Although there is tremendous flexibility with regard to the specific ways in which Christians may appropriately live, I believe there are five basepoints that are essential to the life-style of every Christian—although the specific forms they take may widely vary. These five basepoints are worship, spiritual discipline, community, service, and study. Each of these is essential to the crafting of Christian identity. If one or more of these elements of the Christian life-style is missing, the construction and maintenance of Christian identity is threatened. In the chapters that follow in this section, I will look at each of these five basepoints in turn. But by way of introduction, as well as imaging a holistic picture of Christian life-style, I wish to highlight in brief form their essence.

Worship

In worship one experiences the sense that one is part of a group which celebrates commitment to the same symbolic forms, as well as that Presence which sacralizes the values announced and recited in worship. Worship is communion—with those who are on the same journey of faith and also with that One who is the source and strength of us all. In worship the collective bonds uniting fellow Christians are renewed; and in worship there is the potential of encounter with that One who affirms, yet challenges and confronts, the very framework of our being. Worship is both a social and a personal experience. The very presence of others who are engaged in the celebration and affirmation of the faith one shares lends personal protection for one to pursue the inward/outward journey (see chapter 6).[12]

Spiritual Discipline

To begin and/or end one's day with prayer, the reading of Scripture, and reflection and meditation is to enclose the world of everyday activities in a context of religious significance. Our response to the world rests upon our perspective, our typification of the situation. To experience this world as the creation of God, to perceive the people we meet and the situations we encounter as the arena of God's activity, requires that we continually seek to mend the cognitive net through which we see the world around us. The spiritual discipline of reading the Psalms or other Scriptures, of giving voice to our gratitude and articulation to our concerns, of examining our motives and contemplating our duties—these are the daily practices that turn the profane world of everyday life into the stage of divine intervention (see chapter 7).

Community

Identity is not crafted in solitude, though solitude may be an essential occasion for self-examination. It is in the community of work and play, of committee meetings and picnics, that identity is forged. We are social beings. We know ourselves, in part, as we see ourselves reflected in the responses that others make to us. We become who we are as we make mistakes, offend others, nurture and care and love those around us. It is in community that private matters become public, that partially articulated fantasies are elaborated, that fears find acceptance, that failures are forgiven and new hope is realized. Community is communion, and therein lies the very essence of the religious life (see chapter 9).

Service

The Christian vision includes the support of private religious experience and the cultivation of community among its members, but it does not rest its case with such inwardness. Just as commitment to causes that transcend the self is the key factor to making personal life meaningful, so also is commitment to serving the needs of those outside the boundary of the church the key to communal fulfillment. Self-centeredness is destructive on both a personal and a corporate level. Both individuals and corporate bodies find (and define) themselves by dying to their own self-interested desires. Self-development as an end in itself is always bound to fail; character is defined and structured in service to others. Perhaps the central contribution of Protestantism to Christianity is the formulation that work within the world is equal in spiritual status to a clerical calling to work within the religious community (see chapter 9).

Study

Life-style is a product of seeing the world in a specific way; hence, every life-style has its corresponding mentality. The "Christian mentality" is potentially crafted in a variety of ways—specifically in worship and through communal interaction—but it is also constructed through immersion in the "forms" (the stories, parables, maxims) that comprise our heritage as a community. The Christian's perception of the world will be culturally unique only to the extent that individual Christians have immersed themselves, through study, in the cognitive framework of the founder of Christianity and of the prophetic tradition from which he issued. One does not have "the mind of Christ" except that one has studied the texts which grant foundation to the Christian Church (see chapter 10).

SOURCES OF CHRISTIAN IDENTITY

If worship, spiritual discipline, community, service, and study are five basepoints of the Christian life-style, then *Scripture, tradi-*

tion, and the inspiration of that one called the *Holy Spirit* are the three sources for the content of these basepoints. The *Bible* is an indispensable guide to the acts and teachings of those with whom we stand in historical continuity and whose experience is normative in guiding our perception of what constitutes an appropriate response to the world. It is in *tradition* that one finds a record of the various attempts to interpret the meaning of the biblical stories; and it is in this tradition that one sees the various experiments by members of the church to attempt to apply their insights to the world around them. Finally, new insights as to the meaning of both Scripture and tradition come only through the instrumentality of the *Spirit.* We are part of an evolving community in which new social and cultural situations call out for new inspiration. We are more than purely a human community as we listen to that Word which comes to us both in our ponderings over the Scriptures and in our study of the history of reflection regarding what it means to be a Christian.

What saves us from fanaticism and the idolatry of making our private revelations into sacred pronouncements is the existence of the community of faith. It is in community that we most appropriately struggle with questions of personal moral concern. It is with the community that we share our inspirations, seeking to distinguish the purely human from the divine elements. It is the community that saves us from the excesses of private fantasy. And it is the community that needs our pronouncements, our prophetic utterances, our correction. There truly is a "holy dialectic" at work in the church to the extent that it channels the quest of its members for ultimacy, while at the same time is goaded by its members to exist less compromisingly within the world.

MARKS OF THE CHRISTIAN

What makes the Christian community a dynamic presence within the world is that her members are a heterogeneous lot united by a core of distinguishing marks. Christians may be rich and poor; they may work in the helping professions and in the world of corporate finance. I suspect they may even be in the military and offer their talents to the defense industry. On one level there is little uniformity of life-style required of Christians: they may or may not eat meat, drive a Mercedes, or live in an expensive neighborhood. It is because of their diversity that they function as leaven within the world. Externally their life-styles may vary widely. Yet I would maintain that some aspects of the following elements must be present internally in each of them or else they seriously misunderstand the good news of the Gospel.

First, the Christian is one who does not live for himself or herself. Identity is found in being the Man-for-Others.[13] *Second,* the Christian is one who finds his or her source of security not in the self (nor in the material world), but in God. Personal value is experienced as deriving from one's status as the creation (the son or daughter) of God. *Third,* the Christian is one whose convictions about the good, the right, and the obligatory are founded upon a sense that these are transhistorical values, rooted in the Ultimate Nature of Reality. Values are not mere social constructions. *Fourth,* the Christian lives his or her life in terms of a vision of the possibilities that exist to make society more just, people more loving, and communities more compassionate. Hope is the hallmark of the Christian; he or she lives believing in the hope of the resurrection in spite of all the despairing evidence to the contrary.

Finally, almost any style of life is possible so long as one stands, at least some moment of each day, naked before a God who is both judge and savior. If we have the courage to be present before God, seeking his mercy and undefensively admitting our failures—desiring his direction in the tasks of the day—then God will create in us his own work, and attempts by ourselves at defining specific life-style norms will appear shallow and pretentious to be sure.

NOTES

1. The best overall review of the concept of life-style is by Heinz Ansbacher, "Life Style: A Historical and Systematic Review," *Journal of Individual Psychology* 23 (November 1967): 191–212.
2. On applying the concept of life-style to the field of ethics, see Donald E. Miller, "Life Style: A Category for the Analysis of Moral Identity," *American*

Society of Christian Ethics, Selected Papers, 1976 (Missoula, Mont.: Scholars Press, 1976), pp. 75–88.

3. See Max Weber, *From Max Weber: Essays in Sociology,* ed. and trans. (with intro. by) H. H. Gerth and C. Wright Mills (New York: Oxford University Press, 1958), pp. 187–194.

4. See Alfred Adler, *The Individual Psychology of Alfred Adler,* ed. (and annotated by) Heinz L. Ansbacher and Rowena R. Ansbacher (New York: Basic Books, 1956; Harper Torchbooks, 1967), pp. 172–202.

5. See H. Richard Niebuhr, *The Responsible Self: An Essay in Christian Moral Philosophy,* with intro. by James M. Gustafson (New York: Harper & Row, 1963), pp. 149–178.

6. In this regard, see James Gustafson, *Christian Ethics and the Community* (Philadelphia: Pilgrim Press, 1971), pp. 165–176.

7. See William James, *Pragmatism, A New Name for Some Old Ways of Thinking* (Cambridge, Mass.: Harvard University Press, 1978).

8. See S. J. Levy, "Symbolism and Life Style," in *Towards Scientific Marketing,* ed. S. A. Greyser (Chicago: American Marketing Association, 1963), pp. 140–150.

9. See Thomas Luckmann, *The Invisible Religion: The Problem of Religion in Modern Society* (London: Macmillan, 1967), p. 86 ff.

10. Will Herberg, *Protestant, Catholic, Jew: An Essay in American Religious Sociology* (Garden City, N.Y.: Doubleday, Anchor Books, 1960), p. 268.

11. Ibid., pp. 254–281.

12. On the theme of the inward/outward journey, see Elizabeth O'Connor, *Journey Inward, Journey Outward* (New York: Harper & Row, 1968).

13. See Dietrich Bonhoeffer, *The Cost of Discipleship* (New York: Macmillan, 1963).

The Moral Significance of Worship

6

ALTHOUGH I believe that worship potentially is an exceedingly important component of the experiences which shape Christian identity, the literature on worship reflects a certain ambiguity as to its specific contribution to the moral life. The very title of Peter Berger's early book, *The Noise of Solemn Assembles*,[1] reflects this sense of the lack of moral challenge that is experienced in the church's gathering together of its people. In this chapter, however, I wish to argue that in spite of a viable critique which may be issued against the linkage between worship and moral experience, there is an important case to be made for the vital role which the worship experience potentially may play in positively shaping the moral life.

WORSHIP—A CONSERVATIVE FORCE?

Undoubtedly one place to locate the historic origins of the ambivalence sometimes felt by ethicists towards worship is within the framework of Emile Durkheim's assertion that the object of worship is society: its values and collective sentiments.[2] Obviously such a functionalist perspective casts worship in a very conservative role (i.e., baptizing the values of the dominant culture). It is, of course, also from Durkheim that the notion of a "civil religion" comes, followed in recent times by a number of commentators seeing in such a development a nonheroic, nonprophetic expression of religion.[3]

From another perspective, worship has also been identified as conservative, and that is in the identification of worship with other-worldly mysticism. Although the mystics of the church have almost always denied the charge of narcissism,[4] critics have often viewed mystics as inward, devoid of any real, redeeming social role (however glorious their private ecstatic experiences may be). Countering the mysticism-narcissism conjunction, however, is the witness of numerous powerful figures who have combined the inner with the outer life: not the least of whom in the contemporary period are such "saints" as Thomas Merton and Mother Teresa.[5]

Whatever negative perspective one may have on the moral significance of worship, one must acknowledge the widespread recognition of anthropologists and sociologists that rite and ritual are central to the unity and sustenance of communal experience and therefore not to be lightly debunked.[6] Durkheim stated that it is in the cult that one most clearly feels oneself to be a member of the collectivity. He likewise argued that every group has a need periodically to renew itself through collective rites and rituals.[7] Without ritual assemblage, the autonomous individual lacks a feeling of union with the community. Hence, however cynical some commentators may be about the worship experience, without rite and ritual religious institutions would not long sustain themselves.

Although I do not wish to counter the accuracy of such commentators as Will Herberg and Peter Berger who have critiqued religious institutions for the nonprophetic role they often assume,[8] I do, on the other hand, wish to argue that worship—on four different levels—potentially plays a positive role in the development of the moral life. *First,* moral identity is crafted in community. To the extent that every community is a "moral community,"[9] and to the extent that worship functions as the central incorporative moment within the life of the Christian community, worship and moral identity are closely linked. *Second,* the drama of worship and liturgy serves to image in a variety of ways an ideal moral order in which symbols, metaphors, pictures, and stories potentially exercise a considerable role in providing an individual with a persuasive moral vision guiding lifestyle choices. *Third,* it is in worship that the individual may experience the "otherness" which lends authority and legitimation to the moral vision thus proclaimed. *Fourth,* worship provides the structure, psychologically—through the rites of confession, absolution, and the announcement of "new hope"—for personal moral transformation.

The "mental picture" operant as a reference point in the discussion that follows is the liturgical form of worship practiced in the Anglican/Episcopal tradition. By electing this particular style of worship as a point of reference, however, I do not wish to preclude from consideration more nonliturgical styles of worship. Indeed, I believe there is as much ritual (if not more) in the worship service of a Southern Baptist congregation, or a Pentecostal church, as there is in a Catholic, Lutheran, or Episcopal church. The former may be outwardly less ritualistic, but the worship style itself conforms nevertheless to a highly structured ritual form as regards appropriate and inappropriate behavior, with drama being a not insignificant aspect of the entire experience.

One further qualification is in order. Just as various forms of worship are not homogeneous, likewise the *response* to worship is not uniform. The key term in assessing the moral significance of worship is *intentionality.*[10] The effect and importance of worship to the individual is dependent, first, upon the frame of reference which the individual brings to worship and, secondly, upon the meaning which the individual imputes to his or her experience of worship. Nevertheless, what occurs in the context of worship itself is not unimportant, for "reality" is always created in the dialectical exchange between what is external to consciousness and the filter of expectations brought to an experience.[11]

THE INCORPORATIVE ROLE OF WORSHIP

Moral identity is not structured in social isolation.[12] It is through interaction with particular individuals and through group associations that one's moral identity is formed. Morality is necessitated because individuals exist in a social world, and it is with other people that an individual negotiates his or her view of what constitutes appropriate social and personal relatedness. The significance of the Christian community is that traditionally it has been one of the central repositories and promulgators of a specific value position; membership in the Christian Church implies, as was argued in the last chapter, one's commitment to an identifiable style of life and a set of value commitments. In worship these values are announced and one is invited to join in their celebration and in the acknowledgment of the wellsprings from which they originate and by which they are sustained. Worship is certainly not the only context in which values are internalized, but for some individuals—for whom the religious community is a primary reference group—worship is the central moment in their lives for systematic moral challenge. And that is as it should be.

Participation in corporate worship brings one into the symbolic frame that governs communal existence, thus potentially influencing personal attitudes, dispositions, and proclivities toward action. In any assemblage there is a considerable incorporative power in the very presence of a group of people who are united in a common act. Studies in "mob psychology," for example, demonstrate repeatedly the power of a group to enclose in its ranks those who are on the fringe or periphery. A man may stop to watch a demonstration or rally, and before long someone has struck a picket sign in his hands and he is shouting and marching with the throng, a convert to the movement. Something not unlike this process can happen in worship, to a greater or lesser degree. There is an incorporative power in the liturgy: in the group confessions of faith, the singing of songs, the corporate recitations, and so on—each of which invites the individual to become part of the community. It is as one participates in these acts that one feels oneself becoming more a part of the collectivity. Internally this process may be experienced as the feeling: "These are *my* people, *my* group, *my* tribe; this is where I belong."

As part of worship there may be rather specific incorporative rites and rituals that signal to the individual and to the community one's decision to affiliate with the group. Baptism and confirmation rites are, of course, the most common examples within Christendom, although every religious tradition has its equivalent rites of passage.[13] These ceremonies are milestones in that they symbolically mark one as a member of a particular community. Such *stigmatizing* acts are important because they provide one with a social identity. The collectivity into which one is initiated becomes a reference group to the individual, and individuals within the group function as "significant others" to the new member. While performing the acts of membership, the individual acquires specific reference points for personal behavior and development.[14] In short, in facing specific moral quandaries, the group (and individuals within it) may function in an "ideal observer" role, guiding what constitutes an appropriate moral response.

In addition to specific incorporative rituals, such as baptism and confirmation, there are other collective acts that serve to unite the individual with the community and with the tradition within which members of the community stand. One of these acts is the collective recitation of creeds. Within Christendom, to say the Apostles' or Nicene Creed is to affirm that there is a common symbolic core which all members of the community share. Even if this common symbolic core is recognized as mythic, the impact of sharing a common "story" is unifying. In parallel fashion, Scriptures that are read—again, regardless of whether they are interpreted as fact or myth—elaborate the common ground of those who stand within the tradition.

The importance of labeling oneself as belonging to a specific tradition or religious community cannot be underestimated. Morality is not cultivated in the private sphere so much as it is arrived at through one's interaction with others, through identifying oneself as being "this" and not "that."[15] The very act of typifying oneself as belonging to a particular group establishes an identity that carries with it certain expectations.[16] Every group is organized around specific shared sentiments, and thus group membership necessarily implies that one possesses (at some level) a "moral identity" insofar as every group is (at some level) a "moral community."

MORAL VISION IN WORSHIP

Theology and ethics, description and prescription, are almost always intertwined in worship. In everday life, the so-called naturalistic fallacy (mixing prescription and description) is regularly committed.[17] Moral prescriptions flourish in great abundance in worship, and often they are paired with statements about the nature of God, the nature of the human, what portends for the future, what has gone on in the past, and so on. One side of these prescriptions is inevitably stated negatively as prohibitions. But another and perhaps more important dimension of the moral significance of worship is the range of positive images of what life *can* and *should* be. Worship services are often highly successful at conjuring affirmative images—of peace, love, justice, and a host of other positive mental pictures of what social existence might be. Robert Bellah states: "There is a natural movement from liturgy, which is communion, to brotherhood, to caring and curing, to social concern. . . ."[18]

In the Christian community, Jesus is the symbolic form onto which moral virtues are projected and through which the Christian understands his or her ethical responsibilities.[19] But Jesus is not the only symbolic form present in the context of worship. Not insignificant is the ambience created through architectural forms: the beauty of symmetrical arches, the luminescence of stained-glass windows, the smooth and worn feel of polished mahogany. Such architectural expressions share a congruence of spirit with the prodigious organ and choral works that fill these cavernous stone and wood forms. But perhaps central in many worship contexts is the focus on the verbal expressions present in the sermon. It is in the spoken word that "mental pictures" of specific moral ideals are imaged. The Christian tradition is filled with stories, parables, and biographies that admit to elaboration and revivification.

The function of images in worship is predicated upon the assumption that we are symbolic animals, ones who understand ourselves through images, stories, and myths.[20] Although our symbolic capabilities permit us to think abstractly and propositionally, we reflect largely in pictures and images (as indicated by the rich repository of images latent within every religious tradition). These pictures have evocative power, as opposed to simply rational persuasiveness. For example, in Christendom, to talk about being "like Christ" clearly has meant to imitate the mental picture one has of the earthly Jesus. The idea of a Messiah, or of a coming Kingdom, has equally obvious evocative power as a result of the image which is conjured.

The importance of these images is that they potentially become the guiding line (what Alfred Adler called later in his career "fictional goals")[21] by which individuals make life-style decisions. They give direction to life. They provide ideals for which one may strive. They influence life-style choices insofar as they enable us to picture holistic models of what it means to be truly human. There is a sense in which propositions about what is bad, wrong, or prohibited do not give the same overarching direction to life as do exemplary biographies or utopian social images (e.g., the "picture" of the faith of Abraham, or the "image" of the lion lying down with the lamb).

In the parables and stories of almost every religious tradition one finds dramatized the universal conflicts of life. One sees in picture form the battles between good and evil and the struggles of individuals to contend with themselves, God, and those around them. Such images permit personal identification in the present with these historic personages, their problems—and their resolutions—and hence such stories perform an important role in providing universal paradigms (known collectively by those in the community, and thus enabling a common moral discourse) upon which one may project one's personal struggle.

The achievement of the worship experience is contingent upon the degree to which it allows one to view the world differently as a result of participating in the drama of the liturgy. Within worship one is invited to look upon life with different eyes. One is invited to see "God's hand" in the events that greet one in the morning newspaper. One's personal existence is said to have meaning beyond the pragmatic problem of survival. A cosmic perspective is superimposed upon the everyday world, and one is encouraged to respond to the world as the creation of God. To so perceive the social and physical world (as God's creation) is to imply a particular moral response, one in which the task of life is to live according to the divine will, rather than one's own.

A LEGITIMATING PRESENCE

On the level of purposeful intention, many individuals would state that the express reason for worship is to praise and glorify God. In the discussion heretofore our attention has focused primarily on the latent, as opposed to express, functions of worship. It would be inappropriate, however, to lose sight of the expressly theological dimension of worship as experienced by those who engage regularly in worship. People come to worship to praise God, to "sit" in his presence, to beseech him, to celebrate what he has done in the community and in their own lives. Furthermore, individuals report that they *feel* God's presence while worshipping. The ways in which such experiences of the divine may be understood are, of course, subject to manifold interpretations, but I believe it is important to be both phenomenological as well as pragmatic at this point; if an individual feels that he or she experiences God, then God is *real to that person,* and his or her life is correspondingly affected.

The importance of the experience of the *mysterium tremendum* in worship[22] is that its "otherness" lends authority, or one might say a "legitimating presence," to the ethical vision presented in worship. The moral demands presented in the liturgy, the sermon, and so on, are potentially subject to objectification: perceiving these pronouncements to be of nonhuman (godly) origin and, therefore, possessing ultimate authority.[23] From the perspective of behaviorism, one might view this process as conditioning through "paired association," because the individual's experience of "otherness" is associated in time and space with a particular moral vision and set of pronouncements. As a result, both the moral vision and the pronouncements become imbued with a sacred quality. In other words, the worshipping individual may be likely to associate his or her entire experience within worship as participation in the realm of the sacred; thus the moral pronouncements announced in worship are also baptized with a certain otherworldly (sacred) facticity.

It is outside the sociologist's or psychologist's purview as to whether or not what the individual experiences is to be identified as *real;* subjectively, it is real to the one who claims it to be, and consequently it affects his or her behavior in a corresponding manner. The moral significance of one's experience of the sacred within worship is that potentially one "sees" things differently (to the extent that one believes there is another reality beyond that of everyday consciousness). The altered vision in which, for example, one "sees through the eyes of Christ" is contingent upon an affirmation that there is another dimension (or perspective) which can transfigure the purely material conception of everyday activities. In his *Report to Greco,* Nikos Kanzantzakis related the words spoken to him by a monk at Sinai: "One morning you will rise and see that the world has changed. But you will have changed, my child, not the world. Salvation will have ripened in you."[24] H. Patrick Sullivan states that the fall of man was the move into a divided consciousness in which he was no longer able to see the rootedness of all things in the sacred. In worship it is possible to transcend this dividedness as the individual experiences a union between himself or herself and what he or she perceives to be the very ground of existence.

THE RITES OF TRANSFORMATION

In worship the potential for transformation of personal consciousness is related to three occasions within the liturgy: *confession, absolution,* and various *affirmations* of "new life." Psychologically, these three occasions in worship form a perfect triumvirate as regards moral change: first, the individual admits to the moral transgressions and failures of the past; second, the individual is freed through absolution (or forgiveness) from the guilt of these failures; and finally, he or she is offered a vision of hope for a new direction in life. For worship to deal with only one or two of these areas, without the third in tandem, circumvents the complex unity of the psychological process within which these three elements of liturgy evolve. Moral transformation implies "death" to the *old ways* in order that "birth" may be given to a *new way* of life. Absolution, however it is experienced, is the central moment standing between confession and a vision of new possibilities in the future.

These three moments in worship, of course, have their parallels in the transformative process of psychotherapy. The patient (or client) "confesses" to the therapist or psychiatrist the failures of his or her past; the therapist "absolves" him or her by accepting these confessions in a nonjudgmental fashion; finally, the therapist attempts with the patient to build a new, less destructive pattern for the future. In one sense, there is nothing novel about psychotherapy: the therapist is repeating the priestly function with few changes except a modernized vocabulary and the substitution of a couch for a pew.[25]

The power of worship lies in its regularity. Week after week, one is confronted with the occasion to recognize both those things "which one has done" as well as "those things which were left undone." Week by week, one is granted forgiveness. And week by week, one is invited to a new wholeness of being. Although it is possible that such recitations are done unthinkingly, by rote, it is also a possibility—and for many individuals, a reality—that the regularity of worship serves to maintain the individual in a continual state of moral tension. In worship the filter through which one views the world is regularly challenged, amended, and revitalized. The "real" and the "ideal" are brought face to face with each other, and the occasion for symbolic reordering is provided. Old images are discarded and give way to new images; past ideals are replaced with new models.

Within this framework, perhaps the transformative power of the "Confession of Sin" (The Book of Common Prayer, 1979) can be better appreciated.

> Almighty and most merciful Father,
> we have erred and strayed from thy ways like lost sheep,
> we have followed too much the devices and desires of our own
>   hearts,
> we have offended against thy holy laws,
> we have left undone those things which we ought to have done,
> and we have done those things which we ought not to have done.

These words are followed by a statement of absolution. The impact of making such a confession, however, is surely to place the reciter in a state of moral tension, to remind the reciter of the disparity between what he or she affirms mentally and what he or she practices.

The various "Collects" likewise function to remind the individual that he or she does not live unto himself or herself. Note, for example, the "Collect for Guidance" (The Book of Common Prayer, 1979).

> O heavenly Father, in whom we live and move and have our being:
> We humbly pray thee so to guide and govern us by thy Holy Spirit,
> that in all the cares and occupations of our life we may not forget

thee, but may remember that we are ever walking in thy sight; through Jesus Christ our Lord.

What is important in such a statement is the implication that life operates on more than one level. If one elects to be a part of the Christian community, then one does not live on the purely pragmatic plane; one lives "in God" and "through Christ"—however this experience may be symbolized in one's consciousness.

NOTES

1. Peter L. Berger, *The Noise of Solemn Assemblies* (Garden City, N.Y.: Doubleday, 1961).
2. Emile Durkheim, *The Elementary Forms of the Religious Life,* trans. Joseph Ward Swain (New York: Free Press, 1965).
3. See Russell E. Richey and Donald G. Jones, eds., *American Civil Religion* (New York: Harper & Row, 1974).
4. Evelyn Underhill, *The Essentials of Mysticism* (New York: Dutton, 1960), pp. 25–43.
5. See, for example, James Thomas Baker, *Thomas Merton, Social Critic; A Study* (Lexington: University Press of Kentucky, 1971); Malcolm Muggeridge, *Something Beautiful for God: Mother Teresa of Calcutta* (Garden City, N.Y.: Doubleday, Image Books, 1977).
6. Ronald Grimes, "Ritual Studies: A Comparative Review of Theodor Gaster and Victor Turner," *Religious Studies Review* 2, no. 4 (October 1976): 13–25; Hans Mol, *Identity and the Sacred* (New York: Free Press, 1976); Sally F. Moore and Barbara G. Myerhoff, eds., *Secular Ritual* (The Netherlands: Van Gorcum, 1977).
7. Durkheim, *Elementary Forms,* p. 240 ff., 475.
8. Will Herberg, *Protestant, Catholic, Jew: An Essay in American Sociology* (Garden City, N.Y.: Doubleday, 1955), p. 263 ff; Berger, *Solemn Assemblies,* pp. 97–104.
9. Emile Durkheim, *The Division of Labor,* trans. George Simpson (New York: Free Press, 1964), p. 26; Ernest Wallwork, *Durkheim: Morality and Milieu* (Cambridge, Mass.: Harvard University Press, 1972), pp. 75–119.
10. See Maurice Natanson, *Edmund Husserl* (Evanston, Ill.: Northwestern University Press, 1973), pp. 84–104.
11. See Alfred Schutz, *The Phenomenology of the Social World,* trans. George Walsh and Frederick Lehnert (Evanston, Ill.: Northwestern University Press, 1967), pp. 45–96.
12. See Herbert D. Saltzstein, "Social Influence and Moral Development: A Perspective on the Role of Parents and Peers," in *Moral Development and Behavior,* ed. Thomas Lickona (New York: Rinehart and Winston, 1976), pp. 253–265.
13. See Arnold van Gennep, *The Rites of Passage,* trans. Monika B. Vizedom and Gabrielle L. Caffee (London: Routledge and Kegan Paul, 1909).

14. Robert K. Merton, *Social Theory and Social Structures* (New York: Free Press, 1968), pp. 279–440.
15. See Bryan Wilson, "Them Against Us," *Twentieth Century* 172, no. 1017 (Spring 1963): 6–17.
16. Alfred Schutz, *On Phenomenology and Social Relations,* ed. (with intro. by) Helmut R. Wagner (Chicago: University of Chicago Press, 1970), pp. 116–122.
17. On the controversy surrounding the naturalistic fallacy, see Gene Outka and John' P. Reeder, eds., *Religion and Morality* (Garden City, N.Y.: Doubleday, 1973).
18. Robert N. Bellah, "Liturgy and Experience," in *The Roots of Ritual,* ed. James D. Shaughnessy (Grand Rapid, Mich.: William B. Eerdmans, 1973), pp. 217–234.
19. See H. Richard Niebuhr, *The Responsible Self: An Essay in Christian Moral Philosophy,* with intro. by James M. Gustafson (New York: Harper & Row, 1963), pp. 149–178.
20. See Ernst Cassirer, *An Essay on Man* (New Haven, Conn.: Yale University Press, 1944); Susanne K. Langer, *Philosophy in a New Key* (Cambridge, Mass.: Harvard University Press, 1942).
21. Alfred Adler, *The Individual Psychology of Alfred Adler,* ed. (and annotated by) Heinz L. Ansbacher and Rowena R. Ansbacher (New York: Harper & Row, 1964), pp. 76–100.
22. Rudolf Otto, *The Idea of the Holy* (London: Oxford University Press, 1950); Mircea Eliade, *The Sacred and the Profane,* trans. Willard R. Trask (New York: Harper & Row, 1957), pp. 8–13 ff.
23. Peter Berger, *The Sacred Canopy* (Garden City, N.Y.: Doubleday, 1967), p. 11 ff.
24. Patrick H. Sullivan, "Ritual: Attending to the World," *Anglican Theological Review* 5 (June 1975): 16.
25. See Thomas C. Oden, *The Intensive Group Experience: The New Pietism* (Philadelphia: Westminster, 1972).

Spiritual Discipline—Countering Contemporary Culture

7

Ours is an age of confusion, as evidenced by the burgeoning of the field of clinical psychology. A considerable percentage of the American population feels unsettled, restless, anxious. Depression is more common than the flu. Many people are frantically active, but lack direction, purpose, and meaning nonetheless.[1] How many acquaintances can anyone of us name whom we genuinely respect because of their character and integrity, because they are peacemakers in the world and hence have a sense of peace with themselves? Which heroes and heroines of this age last beyond the duration of their cover photo on *Time?* There is temporary ecstasy, yes—but long-term satisfaction? Only for a few. Ours is a pluralistic culture, heterogeneous and confused. Alternative life-styles, a multitude of choices—but no center of values, no depth dimension to life, no awareness of the fixity of moral norms. It is in this setting that we live and have our being.

It seems to me that several options confront us. First, we can slip from one fad to the next, from one to another commitment induced by the media and the consumer industries. Jogging, racketball, roller-skating, Perrier-sipping, swinging—what's next? Just keep on moving! To live from one job promotion to another—that seems to be the antidote for wondering what it all means. The highest values of our culture, at least as portrayed in the media, seem to be these: "getting it on" and "keeping it up" and figuring out what to do next. Breadth, but little depth.[2]

A second option is to plod along, a little bewildered at what is going on around us, but certain that we don't want to be a part of it. We sense no particular moral self-consciousness—except for tradition, the way things have always been done. Dismayed, a little depressed, but plodding on: holding institutions together and making certain that the mail gets delivered and that the stock market doesn't go too low. One might even conserve a little on energy. Television presents the larger moral challenges of the week—trying to find the worthwhile programs.

A third option—the way of many liberal Christians—is to pay our tribute to the church, the YMCA, the League of Women Voters; to be responsible, read the newspaper; to remember birthdays and worry about our children's future. The guilt evoked on Sunday morning may actually make us feel better rather than worse. Religion is a part of our life, but not at its center. We are moral in a conventional sort of way, but not exemplary. In life-style we resemble the rest of the people in our corporation or profession.

But there is a fourth option, and we may even have toyed with it; but perhaps we were uncertain about how to implement it, or about whether we would really find it desirable. This option makes one's religious identity central to the myriad of other identifications one may possess. Under this option, life becomes more difficult rather than easier, but it also has the potential for becoming correspondingly more ordered, more meaningful, more satisfying. One exercises one's freedom in order to lose it. As the biblical paradox goes: in losing one's life, one also may find it.[3]

THE LIBERAL CONDITION

Although on one level the typology of alternatives given above may sound trivial, even trite and hackneyed, nonetheless it is valid. I strongly suspect, however, that only out of a great sickness of heart, a considerable sense of need, can any of us seriously approach the fourth option. We have grown tired of the latest fad and seek something more enduring (option one). We have become depressed with the lack of intensity and depth in our commitment to life (option two). We realize that, in any meaningful way, we lack identity, and we seek union with that which will give us a sense of ultimate fulfillment (option three).

So the only one left is option four, but it produces fear at the same time that it offers promise. Why? Because it involves a level of commitment which for most of us has not been tested.

I believe that the instrumentality whereby we establish an identity that is self-consciously "Christian"—an identity to supersede all others—is a firm commitment to a daily spiritual discipline of meditation and prayer, with the study of Scripture and religious history occupying a not-insignificant place in our lives. At this point, however, I want to dissociate what I am arguing from fundamentalism. I am not arguing for a commitment to biblical literalism, or to magical notions of prayer, or to nonintellectual/nonintrospective meditation. I do wish, on the other hand, to articulate a rationale for liberal Christians to engage in activities that have in fact largely fallen within the territory of their conservative fellows.

There is surely a place for the liberal Christian to let his or her light shine alongside those representing a more conservative temperament. It is time for Christians of a liberal bent to show unashamedly their commitment to a life-style informed by reason, rooted in contemporary culture, enhanced by the arts, *and* inspired by that mystic Wonder which exceeds formulation in precise doctrinal statements or moral legalisms. Liberal Christians need to look to their past for examples of those individuals who had a commitment to social justice, pursued intellectual inquiry, *and* lived lives noted for piety.[4]

With a few outstanding exceptions, liberal Christianity is in the doldrums. Liberation theologians evoke a few gasps of guilt from North American audiences, but the inner reserves of liberal Christianity are largely depleted, drained by too much secular theology and too many radical theologies, and not enough nourishment at the fount of religious experience.

THE DISCIPLINE OF PRAYER

As liberal Christians we worship, often grandly, and organize for social action; we furnish most of the creative theologians and biblical scholars—or at least we used to; but we seldom encounter personally, as we did in the past, the Source of our reflections. Either we're too busy, or we've read too much Freud. Yet perhaps we should heed William James's words that prayer is the very essence of the religious life.[5]

Many liberal Christians have grave difficulty in knowing exactly in what sense God is personal. This difficulty is not insignificant, because the personal character of God determines the meaningfulness of prayers that request God's intervention in our lives and in the affairs of human history. I submit, however, that we have no right to pronounce on God's personal or impersonal nature unless we have explored the depths of being through the discipline of prayer. If after a season of our life has been spent in prayer and God is still a nonpersonal being, then let our pronouncements ring forth, but not until then.

Above all, prayer is an act of articulation—of speaking forth those concerns, feelings, and attitudes that are most fundamental to our being. Praying allows us to give words to feelings which otherwise may lie unspoken. Articulation of concerns is cathartic. To have no outlet for expressing our thankfulness for existence, for the beauty of creation, for the peace that resides within our own hearts and at times within the world—such a lack would lead to a withering of the human spirit. Prayer allows us to feel our connectedness to all of creation. And whatever else God may or may not be, God is at the center of the reality of existence. Hence, perhaps the question of whether God is personal or not is not to be answered on a rational level so much as on an experiential level. Can we not say that as Christians we should pray because in this way we communicate our solidarity with the creation that we believe to be sustained and created by God?

Prayer is not an act of beseeching a magical power for answers to our requests. Rather, it is an act in which we voice our deepest concerns—realizing that to articulate these concerns is to participate in that existential drama of affirming life over death. God symbolizes the source of life and of human creativity. To pray is to focus our concerns for human wholeness and to acknowledge our thanks for the expression and potential of new life that may arise in place of that which is broken, shattered, and dissolute. In prayer we affirm that being dominates over nonbeing.[6]

God does not, I suspect, need our prayers. Prayer is a *human* activity, and thus it may be humanly understood. When we pray for personal guidance and direction, we are affirming to ourselves (and in the case of group prayer, to others) our intention to live in such a way that justice, peace, and truth might prevail. When we pray for others, we are stating our desire to uphold and, with the whole human creation, participate in the act of bringing good out of evil, life out of death. As articulation of our deepest concerns, prayer shapes our perceptions of the world and our duties within it and hence may even provide the context for a self-fulfilling prophecy.

In prayer we acknowledge our dependence upon the source of all life, God. We affirm our desire to be co-creators with God—an act that in itself shapes a consciousness which is receptive to perceiving God's will for us as we participate in the drama of religious existence. To disavow prayer as a part of one's everyday experience is to cheat oneself of that gracious gift of giving voice and form to that which otherwise is shadowy and without shape, inchoate in perception. Prayer provides an instrumentality for reformulating our attitudes toward events and circumstances, and permits a forum for confessing our failures and stating our commitment to personal renewal. And perhaps most important, prayer saves us from arrogance as we regularly acknowledge that the source of all being is not within ourselves. That in itself makes prayer a worthwhile endeavor.

CHRISTIAN MEDITATION/CONTEMPLATION

Meditation is of two broad types: that which seeks to block out the reality of the external world, and that which seeks to still the mind in order to attend to the internal and external realities. The first searches for enlightenment through the experience of nothingness; the second searches for fulfillment by responsibly attending to the worlds around and within one. Christian meditation is of the second type; it is active and content-filled. Its practice, however, may be of a passive nature. The value of meditation within the life-style of a Christian lies in its opening us to realities that are covered over in the flow of a life of activity.[7]

The moral life of an individual is governed more by his or

her self-image and self-conception than by any list of proscriptions and rules. It is in contemplative periods that an individual gains heightened awareness of who he or she is. Insights into the self surface in the quietness of meditation, insights which everyday consciousness normally shields from awareness. It is in contemplative moments that perceptions of self and duty may be realigned, that new aspirations are formulated, life plans established, goals set for the day, the week, the year. In meditation, order may be brought to the chaos of responsibilities and commitments, and priorities reaffirmed or altered.

The admonition to "know thyself" has in recent times been translated primarily into therapeutic contexts where self-knowledge is made an end in itself. For the Christian, that is not so. Self-knowledge is deemed important for the life one lives under the canopy of a commitment to a community of persons seeking to embody specific moral and spiritual ideals. Herein lies Freud's error, as well as his confession—that psychoanalysis promises only greater freedom, not greater happiness.[8] Similarly, meditation/contemplation is not an end in itself for Christians, but a means leading to better embodiment of the ideals which mark one's life as a Christian.

The identification of the Protestant work ethic with Christianity is a grave misfortune in many ways. As a result, activity (work in itself) has become more important than the end (happiness, peace, or whatever) for which one engages in that activity. We are busy people, often valuing work, power, and expansion more than we do purpose, integrity, and character. It is no trite saying that the emphasis on the quality of life has tragically been replaced by a stress on the quantity of life.

Meditation can be a shield against the pressures of the dominant society and an assertion of a life-style that is distinguished by the ordered, reflective way in which one pursues goals toward a purpose beyond personal power and self-enhancement. Those who begin and/or end each day in a period of quiet reflectiveness cast their shadows on the affairs of life in a distinctive way, one that is markedly different from the shadows cast by those who rush from one commitment to another, unaware of any end higher than efficiency and "success."

THE BIBLE: NORMATIVE IMAGES

Pure reflectiveness can become a circular experience unless it occurs in some valid framework. For the Christian, at least one basepoint for all reflection and meditation is the symbolic forms present in Scripture and the traditions of the church. In the study of Scripture one learns, or refreshes one's acquaintance with, those stories which make reference directly or indirectly to all the grand questions surrounding human existence.

The Bible is not unique in this regard; other religious traditions possess scriptures that address questions of death, suffering, the good life, and the good society. But since Christians have elected to identify themselves with a particular community and tradition, rather than simply become persons of the "world," the Bible stands as a normative basepoint. One's reflection on human existence is grounded in the context of the biblical stories. Regardless of individual interpretation, there is little dispute that the biblical text does indeed set forth the normative images against which the Christian must seek to measure himself or herself.

Indeed, one mark of the Christian is that he or she faces moral decisions in terms of the normative images present within the tradition. Though Christianity is not a rule-oriented religion, to believe that it is without normative images is a serious misinterpretation. While great freedom is to be found within the Christian life, not everything is permissible; one cannot align Christianity with the individualistic ethic of "doing your own thing." A common adage would have it that almost any sort of behavior can be justified through scriptural reference, but only for the "proof-texter" is this true. Attention to the whole of Scripture results in distinct ideas of the Christian's responsibility in the world. Further, reference to the record of the church and its theologians is immensely instructive in helping one discern specific applications of responsible Christian behavior.

The value of regular scriptural study becomes evident when one is faced with a moral dilemma; one's imagination is—potentially, at least—filled with specific biblical images, virtually a symbolic forest within which to consider a normative answer to the dilemma. Scripture seldom dictates the specific answer to complex contemporary social issues, but it does provide a framework for discussion. In addition, the goals established by the regular Bible reader and the priorities set daily and weekly will be informed by this immersion in the "mind of Christ."

Against the images of the good life presented on television and available in the mass media in general, the Christian must always superimpose the life of Christ and the vision of the Old Testament prophets. Although the historical Jesus is an elusive figure, there are certain normative images of authentic existence which continually manifest themselves in the text of the Synoptic Gospels. And to the reader of the prophetic books of the Old Testament there are recurring images of what constitutes the good society. Christianity will be regarded as a permissive, nonnormative, "do your own thing" religion only by those who never bother to read the Scriptures.

The fact that much of the Bible is couched in mythical language and conceptuality detracts not one bit from its significance for the moral life. What makes the Bible important is neither literalness nor historicity, but rather the images, as represented in story and parable and example, that challenge the moral imagination.[9] Is fantasy literature any less morally challenging than biography? I doubt it. The poverty of the church, however, is that few liberal Christians are sufficiently immersed in the Bible's imagery. A Marxist image of the exploited laboring class is probably more vivid for many than is that of the Good Samaritan. Following the liberal tradition, we are well acquainted with contemporary literature and science—and this is a great strength, not to be abandoned. But I suspect we too easily lose our self-consciousness as Christians through our benign neglect of the Scriptures.

FINDING SUPPORT

Although Christians may in most aspects of their being resemble those who are not Christians, their lives nonetheless should bear some sort of distinctive mark. Specifically, the Christian's rationale (justification) for living in a certain way will differ from that of non-Christians—even if the two life-styles are identical. That the Christian is in this world but not of it means that he or she will participate in society for reasons that supersede purely pragmatic considerations. Living under the utopian judgment of the image of the Kingdom of God, the Christian must always possess a countercultural mentality (employing that term in its larger meaning).

The ideals fostered in private study and meditation can be successfully maintained only if one is supported by significant others who exist in reference groups to which one aspires or belongs.[10] Identities are always a matter of social negotiation.[11] If one is to pursue a self-conscious identity as a Christian, then it is important to meet regularly with fellow Christians for study, reflection, and prayer. In such settings the insights of private meditation may be tested, and colleagues in the faith become bonded together. Shared experiences of reading a novel or studying theology and the Scriptures or praying—these can be exhilarating moments for catalyzing collective identity. Within such settings one allows significant others to influence who one is essentially.

Within such small groups, which are a natural complement to solitary meditation and reflection, moral character and ideas are formulated. We are social beings who need the affirmation of others to live out a countercultural existence. If we are to develop a unique style of existence in a pluralistic world, it will be necessary to be in intimate fellowship with those who are on the same journey. The liberal Christian needs to rediscover the importance of religious retreats, of sanctuaries where study and conversation can occur unhurriedly. But the values gained from such short-lived experiences of withdrawal from the world will be sustained only if one has pledged oneself to a daily personal discipline. Coming to grips with the lifelong task of *being* a Christian can happen only in the solitude of private moments of reflection. Each day presents the dilemmas against which Christian character is formulated.

What does it take to provoke those of liberal temperament to get started on the life of reflection and prayer? To this question I can offer only a personal response. First, I have needed a decade or more to recover from reading Rudolf Bultmann and other biblical scholars. My original and long-standing impression was that if something is not to be literally believed, then it isn't true; thus, there is little reason to study such material in order to effect personal transformation (such a message, admittedly, was not Bultmann's intent). I realize now what a naive view of truth I possessed at that time, but such basic patterns of thought are not easily broken.

Second, to revitalize liberalism we must admit to the frustration and despair of lacking a metaphysically rooted identity. Commitment and identity, as Erik Erikson demonstrated, are integrally tied to ideology—and any ideology we cannot affirm as rooted in the "very nature of things" should not long sustain our attention.

Third, the nausea that results from living in a culture so preoccupied with misplaced values provides the stimulus, I believe, to search for a community where individuals unashamedly give witness to the truth they have found. The beauty of liberal Christianity is that one need not divorce the mind from the body, the emotions from the intellect, the passions from religion, or culture from piety.

In the following chapter we will look at the Christian community as the arena in which the commitments fostered in private become expressed and enacted in public.

NOTES

1. On frantic activity and its sources, see Ernest Becker, *The Denial of Death* (New York: Free Press, 1973), esp. p. 284.
2. The ideal types I am drawing in these paragraphs bear some resemblance to Orr and Nichelson's typology of "expansive man," "savage man," and "conscientious man." John B. Orr and F. Patrick Nichelson, *The Radical Suburb; Soundings in Changing American Character* (Philadelphia: Westminster Press, 1970).
3. Matthew 10:39.
4. Karl Barth lists persons who were both theological liberals and yet had a sense of "spontaneous piety": *The Humanity of God* (Atlanta: John Knox Press, 1979), pp. 16–17.
5. William James, *The Varieties of Religious Experience: A Study in Human Nature* (New York: Collier Books, 1961), p. 361.
6. On the dialectic between being and nonbeing, see Paul Tillich, *The Courage to Be* (New Haven, Conn.: Yale University Press, 1952), pp. 155–190.
7. On the life of contemplation, see Morton Kelsey, *The Other Side of Silence: A Guide to Christian Meditation* (New York: Paulist Press, 1976).
8. Philip Rieff, *The Triumph of the Therapeutic: Uses of Faith after Freud* (New York: Harper & Row, 1966), p. 58 ff.

9. Lucy Bragman discusses the role of fantasy in religion in "Religious Imagination: Polytheistic Psychology Confronts Calvin," *Soundings* 63, no. 1 (Spring 1980), pp. 36–60.

10. For a discussion of the concept of reference groups, see Robert K. Merton, *Social Theory and Social Structure* (New York: Free Press, 1968), pp. 279–334.

11. George Herbert Mead, *Mind, Self and Society: From the Standpoint of Social Behaviorism,* ed. Charles W. Morris (Chicago: University of Chicago Press, 1934; Phoenix Books, 1967).

The Nature and Function
of Christian Community

8

ONE OF the most distinctive social changes that has occurred in the last one hundred or so years is the movement from community to society—or what sociologists refer to as the transition from *Gemeinschaft* to *Gesellschaft*.[1] The change is from a social context in which human interaction is personal and intimate (characteristic of the family, guild, and village) to one in which social interactions are impersonal, atomistic, and role-related. Some commentators have celebrated this transition in social morphology.[2] They see communal societies as restrictive and suffocating. Intimacy is a burden; personal freedom is sacrificed for communal support. Other commentators see the alienation and normlessness of modern society as a high price to pay for the right "to do your own thing."[3]

Rather than take sides in this debate, I prefer simply to posit the dilemma posed by modernity: namely, in the United States and most European countries, we have relatively free and open societies that are marked by their pluralism; they are also distinguished among their citizens by a high level of anxiety, insecurity, and felt sense of inadequacy and inferiority.[4] It is from this perspective that I believe one can profitably talk about the nature and function of the church—*as a community*. In a voluntarist society which is filled with many subgroups vying for the commitment of those who comprise mass society, the church is one subgroup among many.[5] However, I wish to show that when compared to other groups and institutions within modern society, it has at least as great a potential for engendering community as does any of its rival competitors.

Although I can feel the attraction of an agrarian, monolithic culture, I see no way of returning to an earlier historical epoch. Nor am I sure I would desire a reversal of the course of history. Given our current cultural condition, I see the most compelling option as being not that of escape, but that of figuring out how to live more humanely in our present social situation. It is at this point that I believe the Christian church is faced with some interesting possibilities. Stated specifically, I see in one's voluntary commitment to the Christian community the possibility of experiencing the intimacy of *Gemeinschaft* while continuing to live within a social order characterized by *Gesellschaft*.

THE EMERGENCE OF THE CHRISTIAN COMMUNITY

Above all else, the Christian Church is a *human* community. It is subject to historical, social, and political forces. It has gone through numerous permutations. It reflects human frailty as well as human genius. The church is, as James Gustafson has identified it, a "Treasure in *Earthen* Vessels."[6] It is made of clay. It bears the imprint of human construction—yet it has the potential of being filled with a substance that is much more eternal than the form which holds it.

From a sociological perspective, the Christian community evolved in a manner that parallels the development of many other historic religions. The community got its start with a charismatic leader, Jesus, whose power of person and message compelled people to follow him. The initial Christian "community" was a band of followers, disciples, who lived out of a common purse and who followed their somewhat anarchical leader because he offered a message of new hope and promise. As Max Weber first suggested and others have further substantiated, charismatic leaders arise in times of social and economic distress.[7] They gain followers because they appeal to the felt needs of individuals, usually the socially alienated. Often they are persecuted and even killed, as in the case of Jesus, by authorities within the dominant culture. Why? Because implicit in their message is a new social order

which obviously threatens the existing leadership.
Many religious movements collapse with the death of their
charismatic prophet. But a few live on—those, especially, which
contain a message that continues to provide answers to the problems of everyday life and the quest for Ultimate Meaning. Such
was the fate of the Jesus-message. After his death, there were
still those who remained loyal. They recited his teachings to
others. The movement grew. A hundred years later there were
fellowships of Christians in many cities. The early Christian
church was indeed fortunate that one of its early converts was
an educated man, later to be named Paul, who took up the task
of theologizing—interpreting the meaning of the Christ-event as
part of God's revelation to humankind.

Initially the church was communistic. People sold possessions
and banded together to celebrate the last supper and to await
the return of Christ. Paul journeyed from fellowship to fellowship
and gave interpretation as well as help in solving the inevitable
"human" problems that arise in any community. As months and
then years passed, Christians settled down for a longer wait for
the apocalyptic end. As is inevitable, social organization developed. Deacons and elders were chosen almost from the beginning.
The Eucharist and other cultic practices became more formalized.
Lives of Jesus were written (i.e., the Synoptic Gospels).

It was not too many years before there were church councils
and debates over creedal statements. And, of course, a professional
clerical class began to evolve: priests, bishops, and so on. By
the time of Constantine (the fourth century) and the official Chris-
tianization of the Empire, the church had evolved a long, long
way from that antinomian clique which had comprised the original disciples. Doctrine now existed in place of aphoristic sayings.
Moral legalisms were starting to erode the purity of Jesus' simplifi-
cation of the law. Justifications were evolved as to why Christians
might bear arms. Religion had almost become a business. Indeed,
it had become political!

Contemporary Christians should not be shocked by such a
course of events. The church is a *human* institution. It obeys all
the laws of routinization and bureaucratization that characterize
other social institutions. The fact that rituals evolved into sacraments is a nearly inevitable process. Reforms characterize the

history of Christianity, as they do the history of every social institution which survives over a long duration. But reforms are always temporary as the processes of change continue unabated.

TYPES OF CHRISTIAN COMMUNITY

Ernst Troeltsch, a contemporary and friend of Max Weber, provided a number of helpful insights regarding the evolution of the Christian community.[8] In his view, the Christian church has since its inception been involved in cultural compromise. But rather than bemoan such compromise, Troeltsch acknowledged cultural accommodation as inevitable. In every new circumstance in which the Gospel is proclaimed, there will emerge a "synthesis of culture" in which the radical claims of Jesus make their compromise. Within limits, compromise is the very essence of relevance.[9] If an institution refuses to change, if it remains a static force, it dies. Such would have been the fate of Christianity.

Instead, Christianity, said Troeltsch, has always been involved in a dialectical process of accommodation and reform. The *sectarian* expressions of Christianity throughout the ages have sought to return to the purity of Jesus' vision as expressed, for example, in the Sermon on the Mount. They have opposed compromising the radical character of the Christian ethic. They have often opposed culture and have withdrawn from contact with the world. They have stressed the essentially voluntary nature of Christianity and the fact that one is not "born" a Christian, but instead must be "born again." Sectarian Christians have created exceptionally intense communities of believers. Friendships have oftentimes been limited to fellow sectarians, and marriage vows prohibit "unequal yoking" with those outside of the fold. To remain a member of a sectarian community requires that one maintain a life of personal purity and doctrinal commitment.[10] The *church* type that Troeltsch contrasted with the sect type is much more assimilated with the culture. Its members adjust their life-style to cultural demands. The churchly ethic is accommodated to allow Christians to live a life fully engaged in the world of commerce and business. The church type is inclusive rather than exclusive—no special conversion experience is required; one may be a member by virtue of birth and place of residence. The church is a bearer of grace and is thus equipped to deal with human foibles, granting pardon. It accepts humanity's lack of perfection.[11]

Troeltsch also identified a third type—that of *mysticism*—which characterizes the Christian tradition. The mystic is usually peripheral to the Christian community—and at the same time parasitic upon it. Salvation is purely personal for the mystic; it is an act of personal inwardness. The mystic is more concerned with the ecstasy of union with God than with correctness of doctrine. Even the historicity of Jesus is unimportant. The mystic tends toward universalism and tolerance of others' beliefs. The mystic is antinomian and nonlegalistic in his ethics.[12]

Other commentators have extended Troeltsch's three types. Some scholars see the *denomination* as an important form of Christian community which differs from that of the sect or church.[13] Other theorists have elaborated further subdivisions of Troeltsch's category of the sect.[14] Still others, H. Richard Niebuhr as an example, have elaborated whole new typologies that draw their inspiration from Troeltsch.[15] For our purposes, such complexities are not important except to note that Christian community comes in many forms and, also, that the process of reform—characteristic of sectarian responses—is always underway.

The theological question to raise about the church as a social institution is whether or not its evolved forms still serve as "vessels" that potentially mediate the sacred. I believe they have that capability and I am not narrowly disposed to say that one vessel is necessarily superior to the others. Different vessels are appropriate to different mentalities. In this regard I follow Troeltsch's lead by emphasizing the relativity of Christian expressions. Other traditions may have a porthole on the truth and the various branches of Christianity may indeed constitute a sacred dialectic at work.

Nevertheless, this relativity should not be taken lightly. *It does not mean that just because the vessels of the Holy are made with human hands that they are therefore unworthy of use.* Quite the contrary. Troeltsch believed that "the Divine Life is not One, but Many."[16] In his view, religious truth is polymorphous rather than monomorphous—it varies in degree rather than kind.[17] I wish to go at least partway with Troeltsch's suggestion that one can more successfully define Christianity *historically,* by way of its many permutations, than *essentially,* stating dogmatically what Christianity should be. In spite of his historical relativism, Troeltsch held on to the notion of a *religious a priori*—that there is a transcendent ground to reality. Indeed, at one point he stated, "To apprehend the One in the Many constitutes the special character of love."[18]

In short, the Christian community has assumed many forms. Liberal Christians have obviously been closer to the church type than to the sect type. Or in H. Richard Niebuhr's classification, they have been more akin to the "Christ of culture" model than to the "Christ against culture" classification.[19] Niebuhr sees the "Christ of culture" type as being inclusive of the Gnostics who found Jesus essential to their faith, but who also reconciled Jesus with the science and philosophy of their time. He also includes Locke, Kant, and Jefferson as representatives of the "Christ of culture" category—as well as Schleiermacher, Ritschl, Rauschenbusch, and Harnack. So the liberal Christian finds himself or herself in good company with a number of notable representatives of the Christian faith.

Nonetheless, like Niebuhr, I feel uncomfortable with identifying contemporary liberalism too closely with the implications of a "Christ of culture" model.[20] Without some tension with culture, Christianity loses its soul. I believe that a revitalized liberalism must discover how to walk the tightrope between Christ and culture without falling into the abyss of contemporary culture, losing sight of the radical vision of the Christian message.

THE TASK OF THE CHRISTIAN COMMUNITY

To keep from being swallowed up by the values of contemporary culture is not easy—particularly as a liberal Christian. If liberal Christianity merely sanctions and gives sacred legitimation to a secular world view, it will grow anemic, a mere extension of culture—truly a superstructure of culture as Marx viewed all religion. The task of the liberal church, however, is much broader. It should function on three levels: personal, corporate, and societal. Some of its functions will be those of comfort and nurture; others will be prophetic, challenging members to self-transcendence. If the liberal church addresses itself as a community to all three levels—to the personal needs of its members, to the corporate needs of the community, and to the social environment of the larger community in which the church dwells—it will be a vital institution, truly fulfilling the role appropriate to the church in contemporary society.

Personal Needs

People seek out membership in a church because they have personal needs. Many of these needs are universal. They desire friendships that pass beyond role definitions. They feel insecure and inadequate. They fear death. They want to feel that there is a purpose in their life. They feel guilty and seek forgiveness. These are not pathologies, they are expressions of the human condition that is common to us all.

The church may meet these needs in a variety of ways. First, because it is an institution, the church can offer people tasks in which they can feel worthwhile and in which they can express their commitment. Second, because it is a community, the church brings people together and thereby enables the formation of friendships. Third, because it possesses a transcendent symbolism, the church holds out to its members the offer of grace and forgiveness; it gives them a cosmic reason to feel significant; it provides linkages to the Ground of Being which both tempers death and offers support to the downtrodden.

The church is a resource in times of crisis. Its clergy are present to offer counsel, to comfort the sick, to bury the dead. The church also celebrates births. It hosts the community in witness of marital vows exchanged. It marks the transitions through the life cycle. It offers inspiration in times of need and form in times of transition. And perhaps most important, the Christian community offers a context wherein the individual may struggle to join the journey of faith in which commitments are owned and meaning and values are ascertained. Its context—the people, tradition, role models, rite, and ritual—offers resources for the crafting of religious identity.

Corporate Needs

A community, by definition, is a collectivity of individuals who share common values, goals, and/or aspirations. If these common sentiments are not celebrated, then the collectivity is unlikely to long sustain itself. Hence, it is necessary for the Christian community to worship, and to worship grandly. Worship is not peripheral to the community; it is central. Social action programs will not long be sustained by a church that does not know how to worship. It is in worship that the community gains its inspiration and makes connection with the Source of those values that it seeks to embrace and promulgate.

The church is a social institution. Furthermore, it is a voluntary association. It rests for its support on the good will of its members. If members are part of the planning and the implementation of programs and projects, then they will support these efforts with their participation and money. Committee meetings are important occasions. It is disastrous for the clergy to think that they could by themselves do it better. The church belongs to the people. Committee meetings are occasions for socializing as well as programming. Through argumentation and conversation a common vocabulary is built and, with it, a shared mentality is developed. Corporate visions are built only as people gather to plan and to hear challenges for a call to action and, in the case of the church, to servanthood.

Societal Needs

The healthy church is a servant community. It finds an outlet for its aspirations, for its deliberations on the good life, by sharing itself and its resources with the community in which it dwells. The healthy church is one that is a light to its neighbors: it not only cares for the needy and dispossessed, but regularly challenges city hall. It places its members in locations of civic importance. It structures regular forums in which issues of social responsibility may be debated.

The vital church is also one that moves beyond debate and seeks to effect changes of social policy so as to enable a more just and peaceable world. It mobilizes its members in marches. It circulates petitions. It encourages members to write and telephone their legislators. It includes generous allocations in its budget for projects that both include and go beyond the local community. In all that it does, it seeks to remind its members that God is Lord and father of all and that we, his people, are his instruments in the world.

THE COMMUNITY AS REFERENCE POINT

Liberal Christians should find in their religious community a spirit and a style of life among the members that create within them a tension with the values of the surrounding world. They should find in the community the friendships and significant others that give them the courage to resist those values inappropriate to the Christian life-style. The church should be a reference point for its members as they engage in their jobs, making decisions concerning corporate policy, as well as while they interact as citizens with the assorted institutions of society. Courage is an important aspect of the Christian life, and it is only because of a strong identification with the community of the faithful that the isolated individual will have the courage to stand against injustice.

NOTES

1. Ferdinand Tönnies, *Community and Society*, trans. and ed. Charles P. Loomis (New York: Harper & Row, 1963).
2. Harvey Cox, *The Secular City* (New York: Macmillan, 1965).
3. See the classic statement on suicide by Emile Durkheim, *Suicide: A Study in Sociology*, trans. J. A. Spaulding and G. Simpson, with intro. by G. Simpson (New York: Free Press, 1951).
4. On the anxiety of modern man, see Rollo May, *The Meaning of Anxiety* (New York: Ronald Press, 1950); also see Rollo May, *Man's Search for Himself* (New York: W. W. Norton, 1953).
5. On the church as a voluntary association, see D. B. Robertson, ed., *Voluntary Associations: A Study of Groups in Free Societies* (Richmond, Va.: John Knox Press, 1966).
6. James Gustafson, *Treasure in Earthen Vessels: The Church as a Human Community* (Chicago: University of Chicago Press, 1961).
7. Max Weber, *The Sociology of Religion* (Boston: Beacon Press, 1964), pp. 46–59; also see Bryan Wilson, *The Noble Savages: The Primitive Origins of Charisma and Its Contemporary Survival* (Los Angeles: University of California Press, 1975).
8. Ernst Troeltsch, *The Social Teaching of the Christian Churches*, trans. Olive Wyon, with intro. by Charles Gore, 2 vols. (New York: Macmillan, 1931).
9. On this point, see Benjamin Reist, *Toward a Theology of Involvement: The Thought of Ernst Troeltsch* (Philadelphia: Westminster Press, 1966), pp. 156–174.

10. On the nature of the sect, see Troeltsch, *Social Teaching,* pp. 691–728, 993.
11. On the nature of the church, see Troeltsch, *Social Teaching,* pp. 201–328, 993.
12. On the nature of the mystic type, see Troeltsch, *Social Teaching,* pp. 729–801, 993.
13. J. Milton Yinger, *The Scientific Study of Religion* (London: Macmillan, 1970), pp. 264–6.
14. See the elaborate typology on sectarianism developed by Bryan Wilson, "A Typology of Sects," in *The Sociology of Religion,* ed. Roland Robertson (London: Penguin Books, 1969), pp. 316–83. Also my review of Wilson: Donald E. Miller, "Sectarianism and Secularization: The Work of Bryan Wilson," *Religious Studies Review* 5, no. 3 (July 1979): 161–174.
15. H. Richard Niebuhr, *Christ and Culture* (New York: Harper & Row, 1951).
16. Ernst Troeltsch, *Christian Thought: Its History and Application,* ed. (with intro. by) Baron F. Von Hugel (New York: Meridian Books, 1957), p. 63.
17. Ibid., pp. 20–21.
18. Ibid., p. 63.
19. Niebuhr, *Christ and Culture,* pp. 45–82, 83–115.
20. Ibid., pp. 108–115.

Going Beyond Moral Impotence

9

ONE ASPECT of the pilgrimage in faith is the journey inward—to that personal center where contact is established with God. The other aspect of the Christian commitment is the journey outward—to serve the human community in all of its diverse manifestations. These two aspects of the Christian life belong together.

Inwardness that never expresses the love of God to others is pure pathology. Outwardness that neglects the resource of inward communion with God risks either exhaustion or self-serving fanaticism. Liberals are wrong when they emphasize social activism to the exclusion of mystic communion. On the other hand, evangelicals and fundamentalists have perverted the Gospel when they equate the whole of the good news with personal salvation.

FRUITS VS. ROOTS

Inward religious experience is the very life source of a strong outward journey. A vital inward experience gives power to one's quest for peace and justice. An ever-present danger in Christianity—and, for that matter, in any religion—is that worship and doctrine can become mere empty forms. William James stated the potential pathology of institutional religion as follows: "Verbality has stepped into the place of vision, professionalism into that of life. Instead of bread we have a stone; instead of a fish, a serpent."[1] He went on to state, "What keeps religion going is something else than abstract definitions and systems of concatenated adjectives, and something different from faculties of theology and their professors. All these things are after-effects, secondary accretions upon those phenomena of vital conversation with the unseen divine. . . ."[2]

Although James stressed the importance of private religious experience, he nevertheless believed that there is a twofold criterion for religious truth: first, philosophical reasonableness, but second, what he called "moral helpfulness."[3] He captured the essence of the religious witness in the phrase: "By their fruits ye shall know them, not by their roots."[4] James had little patience for finely tuned theological distinctions unless they made some pragmatic difference. By way of example, he questioned what possible difference it could make what attributes are assigned to God "if they severally call for no distinctive adaptations of our conduct?"[5]

Outsiders to the Christian community rightly fault those churches that do not exert a moral witness. At least one test of the Christian faith should be a pragmatic one in which the meaning of a Christian's rhetoric is understood in terms of the actions it produces. Such a pragmatic test of meaning reveals the fallacy of logical doctrines and beautiful ceremonies that fail to empower people to self-transcending service. In religion, verbage is all important—if it translates into service.

My commitment to the church is founded, in part, on the conviction that religion has a vital institutional role to play within contemporary society. Of the half dozen or so institutions which comprise every society, religion has a unique function.[6] I have already spoken of Christianity's nurturing and comforting tasks. But the church also has an important task as a social critic. The prophetic role is one of the important contributions of the church to society. Other social institutions, such as the family, education, economics, and politics, all have relatively conservative roles. The church is one institution whose task it is to raise consistently the moral question. In response to every social policy, every institutional and social configuration, the church has the right to ask whose interests are being served, if justice is being accomplished.

OBSTACLES TO MORAL POTENCY

In spite of the church's prophetic mandate, both scripturally and societally, the question arises as to why the Christian church has so often been conservative, a servant of the ruling class, married to the spirit of the age. I believe there are at least four issues to be explored by way of explaining this state of affairs in the contemporary situation. First, the pluralism of modern culture has bred a spirit of *relativism* that leaves many Christians impotent in its wake. Second, on a fundamental level we possess, perhaps by nature, a *corrupt will,* as evidenced in our common tendency to seek our own self-interest over that of the welfare of the whole human community. Third, through all manner of class and racial and neighborhood *isolation* we spare ourselves the experience of encountering those who are in need. Fourth, many of us lack a clearly articulated *ideology* and, as a consequence, are awash in a sea of competing loyalties.

Relativism

At birth we are thrust, in most instances, into a fairly coherent frame of reference. Parents define reality for us. We internalize a world that contains numerous absolutes. There are definite rights and wrongs. Berger and Luckmann state that this is the biggest "confidence trick" ever played on us, because for at least the first few years of life we grow up believing that this is the sole reality—that everyone believes the way we do, that everyone lives by the same rules.[7]

At some point, however, we experience our parents in disagreement, or we encounter another social reality which is different from that which we internalized. We discover that there are other ways of thinking about the world. And then, as we develop and grow, we encounter a more diverse variety of value systems. Eventually, the problem of choosing one of several options faces us.

First, we may maintain that the value system with which we were reared is the only true system and that all the rest are based on falsehood and misapprehension. If we elect this alternative, it is undoubtedly with the support of parents and other significant others who help build a symbolic hedge between us and the rest of the world. Another alternative is to decide that the system of our acculturation is wrong and that we should convert to another value system. This possibility means establishing new friendships and developing a whole new support system. A third, very likely possibility is that we may conclude all value systems are relative, one as good an another, and therefore it is up to us to take our choice or to create our own system. Moral choice is reduced to a matter of aesthetic appreciation—one system is more *pleasing,* more *appealing* than anôther. The process of deliberating rationally about moral problems is reduced to a matter of our *desires.*

It is this third alternative which is becoming increasingly widespread. It first made its appearance in Christian ethics under the name of "contextual" or "situational ethics."[8] When this form of ethics first appeared, many situational ethicists were extremely responsible, although from hindsight it appears increasingly evident that the "new morality" was a response to modernity, to an erosion of confidence in fixed moral principles. Situational ethics, the law of love, and the leading of the Spirit in "the moment" was easily reduced to a will-of-the-wisp, "do your own thing" narcissism. Everything became permissible. It was all a matter of opinion. Your opinion was as good as mine. Respect for the right of other individuals to exercise their freedom became the only absolute norm.

In the churches, this ethic led increasingly to moral paralysis. If morality is all a matter of personal opinion, then it is difficult to mobilize a sustained religious commitment. A small minority of liberal churches stayed faithful to their historic mandate to fight oppression and to proclaim social justice, but many substituted therapy groups for social action committees. Counselors were hired to replace community organizers, and speaking in tongues replaced marching.

Presently, the church is utterly divided on such issues as abortion, busing, and a variety of international concerns. The "liberal consensus" is fractured into one-person stands. Here and there are a few cohesive units of individuals clustered together around the issue of world hunger or the arms race, but percentage-wise, many more people seem to be preoccupied with their midlife crises or their divorces than with issues of social justice.

A Corrupt Will

At this time when there has been a growth in an ethic of self-assertion and self-actualization, it is almost contradictory that, on an increasingly wide scale, people have come to accept that one may not be responsible for one's actions. All is a matter of social conditioning. The most heinous crimes have been attributed to poor child-rearing. Psychiatric evaluations increasingly fill court proceedings. The old-fashioned, indeed existential, notion that you create yourself through self-willed choices has, at least when convenient, been reduced to deterministic theories of behavioristic and psychoanalytic origin. It seems to me that, in modern culture, the concept of "the will" has been lost, a concept which deserves to be resurrected (along with the equally valid concept of "sin").[9] Certainly moral impotence correlates with a loss of the will.

It is a possible and perhaps even more persuasive explanation, however, that the loss of the will is simply a contemporary expression of the ancient theological doctrine of the corruption of the will (i.e., the "fall" of man)—that when given the opportunity, the human proclivity is to choose self-interest over a broader concern for the social good. What appears to be a loss of will then, is simply a failure of moral intention.

Reinhold Niebuhr sided with Augustine in saying that what is evil about man is his will. Men and women choose themselves over God. The greatest sin, thought Niebuhr, is pride: the failure to admit one's creatureliness. What is at fault, according to Niebuhr, is not social structures or social conditions, but man's nature.

Niebuhr was not hopeful that the answer to man's moral condition is more education; such is not the solution to the drive for self-interest. Evil is not due to ignorance (a classical liberal assumption). Evil is rooted in man's very nature. Not even conversion will alter man's nature (a failure in the evangelical's world view). The world will not become perfect by everyone's getting "saved." "Saved Christians" also sin.

The moral impotence of the church, of course, is not a new phenomenon—nor is the fallen nature of the Christian. The church has often been on the wrong side of moral issues. The church has sponsored crusades, sanctioned racial segregation, supported "holy wars," and the list continues ad naseum. For some, of course, such a track record has been the basis for rejecting Christianity. Without excusing any of the evils perpetrated by the church, I would simply note that such activities are evidence for the validity of Niebuhr's doctrine of sin. As a human institution, the church continues to express, on occasion, evidence of the corrupt will of ministers, bishops, and laypersons. Such moral failures should not be rationalized. Indeed, such occasions demonstrate all the more powerfully the need for men and women to commit themselves to the Christian ethic.

Isolation

At the same time that Reinhold Niebuhr emphasized the human proclivity towards self-interest, he also believed that human beings were created in the image of God. He believed that individuals have the capacity to engage in self-transcending acts. In his book *Moral Man and Immoral Society,* he argued that one reason individuals are more often capable of transcending self-interest than are nations in their relations with other nations is that there is room for empathy in interpersonal exchanges. Individuals can feel sympathy, repulsion, remorse in a way that a group, with its impersonal collectivity, does not.[10]

If we are isolated from the poor, the elderly, the lonely, the widowed, the orphaned, those who are hungry, and those who are sick—as most of us are—then it is very easy not only to ignore their plight, but to pass legislation that places them in even worse circumstances. I believe that our moral impotence is related, in part, to the very fact that we do not daily experience the needs of the dispossessed. If we did, I can not help but believe that however corrupt we are by nature, most of us would nevertheless be moved by empathy to share more generously our time, wealth, and creative talents.

I am struck by the profound character of what has come to be called the Golden Rule. "Do unto others as you would have them do unto you."[11] Such a maxim has a very universalizing quality to it; in fact, it resembles Kant's famous categorical imperative. The Golden Rule implies that in every action that we take toward another, we should ask ourselves if under the same circumstances we would want the same thing to be done to us. Jesus' statement of the law of love implies the same idea—that we should love others as we love ourselves.[12] The Christian ethic of love, however, becomes inoperative—or at least is seriously thwarted—if we are isolated from a major population of whom we might ask, if we were in contact with them, whether we would want done to us what we are doing to them.

The reason that Christians should raise questions about living in segregated housing areas, and being removed from the mentally insane and the elderly, is that such social arrangements exclude us on a daily basis from those who need our love. If we never encounter the poor and the infirm, then we will seldom be moved to exercise the law of love.

Ideology

Erik Erikson argued that the identity crisis of late adolescence is both a necessary and valuable developmental stage.[13] He would have in all probability affirmed Peter Berger's view of the "confidence trick" which is part of a child's early socialization. Children do uncritically internalize the world view given them by their parents and certain significant others. It is important developmentally—if a child is to grow into a morally mature adult—to allow the child to question the world view given by its parents. Erikson noted that the most distinctive and creative contributors to human culture have gone through extended "moratorium experiences" in which they turned their backs on parents and friends and struck out to sample and test the world's offerings. However agonizing these experimental periods may be for parents—and even for the one undergoing such a transition of identity—they hold the promise of a highly creative and responsible resolution.

The identity crisis comes to an end as an individual begins to claim—or reclaim, in the case where the individual returns to the value system of his or her earlier socialization—an *ideology* that structures and organizes his or her perception of the world. Commitment to an ideology—a belief system—brings order to chaos. It assigns priority to commitments. It has the potential of energizing one's contribution to society. And in the case of great individuals, their contribution may be a newly synthesized ideology which, drawing upon the experimentation of the moratorium period, has the potential of achieving new heights of insight and moral leadership.[14]

It is potentially pathological, however, stated Erikson, if one's commitment to an ideology becomes *totalistic.*[15] Uncompromising wedding of oneself to an ideology bears the risk of idolatry and carries with it the neurotic quality of emptying oneself into a movement or cause in which all individuality—and therefore personal moral accountability—is lost. Erikson understood the attraction to totalism (for example, the commitment to fascism), yet he did not condone it. Hence, while ideological commitments are an important part of personal moral maturation, one must always question totalism, and one must, of course, question the values implicit in the ideology to which one offers one's loyalty.

In short, a further source of moral impotence in contemporary society is the broad scale "identity diffusion" that has become a hallmark of the most advanced societies. Moral choice is exceedingly difficult when not done from within the context of an ideological framework that provides parameters for thinking about what is right, just, and personally obligatory. The church should not avoid its obligation to keep alive a comprehensive moral view. At the same time, the church should seek to thwart the idolatrous attraction of totalism. In part, this can be done by encouraging the community of the faithful to understand more fully the way in which theology and ethical pronouncements are promulgated. On the other hand, it is important that the members of the Christian church understand the value of seeking moral commitments within a community where belief systems may be fostered and where individuals may encounter structures that assist them in giving order and form to their loyalties.

BEYOND MORAL IMPOTENCE

I believe that the first step in moving beyond moral impotence is commitment to a community of persons who are concerned about issues of moral justice and absolute truth. Individualism may be operative as one stage in the developmental sequence— for example, during the moratorium period—but I do not see it as occupying a permanent status in the life-style commitments of the morally mature individual. For one thing, the isolated individual is morally impotent against unjust societal structures. Also, I believe that it is in community that one best counters the relativism of a pluralistic society.

Communities provide the context in which individuals may engage in moral discourse on a regular basis. The church is a particularly appropriate context for moral deliberation for the following reasons. First, the church is made up of diverse persons with different life experiences, different professional involvements; these persons are of different age groupings and, at least in some instances, of different racial and social class backgrounds. Any moral deliberation within such a context is bound to be dynamic, a variety of views being represented. Second, the church is continually faced with concrete moral problems that require deliberation. Some of these are internal problems revolving around issues of church policy; some are problems raised by particular members of the community; other issues are those presented by the community and world in which the church is located. Third, the members of the religious community are continually encountering the moral perspectives of their clergy (through sermons), of their tradition (through liturgy), and of their Scriptures (through group and personal study). To join a morally responsible religious community is, in effect, a self-styled invitation to seduction: by the moral rhetoric which fills the very air breathed by the members of the socially engaged church. Fourth, an essential dynamic of community life is that it does not allow one "to think without assent" for very long.[16] Decisions are made, policies are announced, organizational plans are made. Sometimes it is only in acting out a moral choice that one becomes assured of its validity—or its error.

In my view the church is one of the very few institutions that provide the dynamics for countering the pluralism, and subsequent moral relativism and moral impotence, of the modern age. It is indeed unfortunate when churches become country clubs or therapy centers. It is equally unfortunate when they limit their sphere of moral interest to issues of private morality. From simply a systemic, institutional perspective, the church has a task to perform. The church's nearest competitor as a morally leavening influence in society is the university. Unfortunately, the university has abdicated its position of moral leadership even more so than has the church.

In conclusion, I foresee an important role to be played by the theologians of the Christian church. I believe it is vitally important to debunk the common view that moral values are simply a matter of personal and social construction, that there are no absolutes. Perhaps it is time for a revitalized natural law. Relativism will only be countered if persons believe that their moral norms are rooted in the very nature of things; that if they violate certain principles, then personal and social life will be less harmonious, less peaceful, and ultimately less fulfilling. Theologians have a task in helping to make such a case.

NOTES

1. William James, *The Varieties of Religious Experience; A Study in Human Nature* (New York: Collier Books, 1961), p. 349.
2. Ibid.
3. Ibid., p. 33.
4. Ibid., p. 34.
5. Ibid., p. 348.
6. On the societal role of religion, see Talcott Parsons, *The Social System* (London: Routledge and Kegan Paul, 1952).
7. Peter Berger and Thomas Luckmann, *The Social Construction of Reality: A Treatise in the Sociology of Knowledge* (Garden City, N.Y.: Doubleday, Anchor Books, 1967), p. 135.
8. James Gustafson gives an excellent discussion of contextual ethics in *Christian Ethics and the Community* (Philadelphia: Pilgrim Press, 1971), pp. 101–126.
9. Karl Menninger, *Whatever Became of Sin* (New York: Hawthorn Books, 1973).
10. Reinhold Niebuhr, *The Nature and Destiny of Man*, vol. 1, (New York: Charles Scribner's Sons, 1964), pp. 16–18.
11. See the discussion of the Golden Rule by Erik Erikson, *Insight and Responsibility: Lectures on the Ethical Implications of Psychoanalytic Insight* (New York: W. W. Norton, 1964), pp. 219–243.
12. See the whole of the Sermon on the Mount in Matthew 5:1–7:29.
13. Erik Erikson, *Insight and Responsibility*, pp. 109–158.
14. Illustrative examples include both Luther and Gandhi. Erik Erikson, *Young Man Luther: A Study in Psychoanalysis and History* (New York: W. W. Norton, 1958), and *Gandhi's Truth; On the Origins of Militant Non-Violence* (New York: W. W. Norton, 1969).
15. Erikson, *Luther*, p. 93 ff.
16. Note the many references to intellectuals in Philip Rieff's *Fellow Teachers* (New York: Harper & Row, 1973). The specific phrase "to think without assent" appears in Rieff, *The Triumph of the Therapeutic: Uses of Faith After Freud* (New York: Harper & Row, 1966), p. 13.

Christian Education in a Pluralistic World

10

MY THESIS IN this chapter is that the purpose of religious education—whether on a Sunday school or adult level—is *identity construction*. Although religious institutions have many functions and goals, the purpose of the educative endeavor of the religious community is to nurture in individuals the formation of a unique and distinctive identity, one that faithfully represents the integrity and historical roots of the community of which one is a member. The failure—for sociological, and not just theological, reasons—of an educational program which invites each person to be his or her own sect is that the religious institution at that point ceases to be a religious *community*. Religion has always placed boundaries on the lifestyle models and thought patterns appropriate to members of the community; communities, by definition, are comprised of individuals who share common goals and attitudes.

A half dozen years ago, "expansiveness" was the hallmark word. Robert Jay Lifton was writing of the "protean" personality, which simultaneously was everything and yet nothing. Liberation was the vogue. The sensitivity cult flourished. And the church was the first to embrace the unleashing of Dionysian powers.[1]

Unbounded experience, however, proved itself to be an unworthy object of worship. Daniel Bell captured well the emergent sentiment:

The ceaseless search for experience is like being on a merry-go-round which at first is exhilarating but then becomes frightening when one realizes that it will not stop.[2]

The importance of boundaries is once again asserting itself. The "therapeutic," among the more thoughtful, has had its day. Identity is not built out of continual release and remission. Freud wisely announced that culture is built on sublimation and repression; personal character, likewise, is defined against boundaries.[3]

CONTEXT

The questions before us are clear: What is there to be believed? What is impermissible? Who are the heroes and heroines to image our aspirations? These are the questions put to us by a pluralistic culture. It is within this context that the Christian educator functions.

Among sociologists of religion there are several broad lines of agreement about the face of contemporary religious life.[4] First, religious monopolies—if there ever were any—are a thing of the past. The more industralized the country, the more pluralistic it is religiously. The individual is met with a smorgasbord of religious alternatives, each serving up a slightly different offering of doctrine, community, and style.

Second, the religious pluralism of industralized societies suggests a marketplace analysis in which authority is granted to the consumer, unlike prior circumstances in which religious institutions were the purveyors of authority. From a relatively early age, individuals choose their religious options, as opposed to being socialized into a single dominant ideology and style of religious community.

Third, pluralism breeds theological and philosophical relativism. In the face of many contradictory truth claims, the individual asks whether anything can be absolute. A jaded relativism is often the response of intellectuals and clerics alike.

Fourth, there is a tendency towards the privatization of religion, with institutional commitments perceived as somehow inauthentic. Personal experience becomes the final authority; reason and tradition are mistrusted.

Finally, religious institutions are viewed as being increasingly isolated from political influence. With the advent of institutional differentiation, the function of religion has been progressively removed from its influence on the educational, familial, and political spheres.

Given this analysis, it is no wonder that Christian educators question the definition of their task. As citizens of their own age, they are often as caught in the pressures of relativism and cultural quandary as the very audience whom they are called on to educate. In an unwitting escape from these dilemmas, many Christian education programs have catered to two human needs: therapeutic release and sociability. For those habituated into church-going, the religious institution was a logical place to meet friends and to seek release from the burdens of everyday living. Religious educators rallied to the demand. They often were well equipped in the art of counseling as well as the requisite organizational skills for carrying out a full social program. Occasionally a prayer would punctuate the event in order to give it religious sanction.

Religious education programs in liberal churches also rose on occasion to a public service level. Speakers from Planned Parenthood, the League of Women Voters, and other assorted agencies were called in to supplement the nightly diet of television news. And of course the omnipresent psychologist was a frequent visitor, commenting in priestly fashion on the problems of living. In all, these programs within the liberal church have often been well attended, interesting, and helpful. But what specifically they have had to do with Christianity few were moved to ask.

The failure of religious education programs which fit the above caricature is that they facilitate a broad cultural amnesia to that cluster of questions which have always been central to the purview of religious communities: How ought I *really* to live? What ultimate meaning might there be to my life? What values should I hold? Part of the context, then, of religious education is that religious education programs in many liberal churches run the risk of obsolescence on the grounds that they fail to address their historic role definition: the cultivation of metaphysically and historically weighted models of how life *ought* to be lived. I assert this on the conviction that, in essence, humans are meaning-seeking beings who inevitably rise to the occasion of asking questions about the true and ultimate nature of this world in which we live. I believe that all people strive, on however primitive a level, for an ultimate context in which to define the worthwhileness of their commitments.

TEMPTATIONS

A variety of temptations face the Christian educator who is prepared to meet the intellectual challenge of enabling individuals to say what it means really to live. The first temptation, perhaps, is to lead individuals into a philosophical morass. The typical sequence of events is that the educator wants to be intellectually responsible, so he takes his students—at least on an adult level— through Kant, Hume, Tillich, Bultmann—all the while laboring to represent them accurately in short compass, but aware that such landmark figures cannot easily be done justice in a nonacademic setting. The general effect of such a course of events is that the audience becomes vaguely aware that traditional religion is in trouble, but they are not quite certain why, or whether or not there is any way out of the morass.

Another temptation is to marry the spirit of relativism. This is the view that one faith is as good as another, that no tradition possesses the final truth—so why bother to know (or teach) one's own tradition, its theological heritage, or the social forms it has inspired? To assume this stance, however—that differences which in the past have divided people will not also in the present prove to be important lines of demarcation—indicates a lack of sociological and historical awareness. Furthermore, the relativism posed by social pluralism does not imply philosophical relativism. Truth claims have as much intellectual integrity in an age of pluralism as they do within a monolithic religious period. The only difference separating the two eras is that the pursuit of ultimates is undoubtedly (and perhaps necessarily) more harried in the present age—a factor too easily dismissed by some sectarian apologists.[5]

A third temptation for the religious educator is to confess (in the spirit of "honesty") his or her own failure to achieve a settled religious perspective (the loss of hypocrisy in public life is an unfortunate travesty of the prevailing therapeutic ethic).[6]

In confessing the ambiguities of one's religious identity, one reflects the contemporary spirit more than one's calling to a unique and priestly vocation. What is ironic is the pride with which some religious educators betray their own confusions. If such confessions were made in the context of a serious religious pilgrimage, they would be a most welcome entry in the religious community. But when they are the confessions of arrogance, one wonders if these religious educators have not matriculated to their positions of responsibility somewhat inappropriately.

Having noted these three temptations facing the religious educator, it is important to acknowledge the half-truth in each. First, Christian education might indeed involve some familiarity with the philosophical and theological debates that circumscribe contemporary religious faith and practice. Second, to make truth claims without some spirit of tentativeness or qualification often reveals a spirit of fanaticism, rather than intellectual and experiential certitude. Third, genuine honesty is to be prized above all; the religious educator who is genuinely in pursuit of the Truth will often be troubled in spirit and mind. A narrow-minded dogmatism is not the counsel of these pages; a well-defined structure to the formation of Christian identity is.

GOALS

The goal of religious education is to enable the individual to achieve a Christian identity which, because of its attention to questions of meaning and purpose, gives perspective and unity of life-plan to the multiple activities in which an individual engages. Stated differently, the purpose of religious education is to create in the Christian an identity that transcends the particularity of the various roles which characterize an individual's life. Many commentators have raised the question of whether there is a "self" which transcends the various roles individuals must necessarily play in a highly differentiated society, or whether one is a mere assemblage of parts. Religious identity is unique because it functions at the interstices between an individual's various roles. From this perspective, the self is always religiously defined; one's religious identity functions at the center of the personality, granting order and meaning to the assorted roles in which one engages. In this view, religious identity is not identical with any single role; it is the integrating factor (often identified with an ideological stance) that binds the individual into a holistic and unified being.[7]

The goal of religious education is not to fortify individuals with information—herein lies its difference with secular education. Rather, the goal is to transform consciousness—a grand task, indeed. The responsibility of the religious educator is to enable individuals to see the world through new eyes, the prisms through which they peer being the structures and symbols of the Christian tradition. Identity is a correlate of perception: as one sees the world, so one is. The goal of religious education, therefore, is to transform perception according to a Christian world view that unites the past with the present and the individual with the anticipated future of the Christian community.

Identity is by definition based upon structure. The religiously inspired self does not weigh all experience equally. Value commitments structure both the projects one enacts and the responses one makes to the world one encounters. As we have seen, Erikson argued that identity is shaped through ideological commitments. Although liberation may be the goal of religious experience, it is achieved through enslaving commitments and, perhaps ultimately, through repression. For it is in conformity to a specifiable hierarchy and structure of commitments that freedom is experienced. Communities are comprised of those who share a common definition of the path to liberation and responsible behavior. To be a member of the Christian community is to be self-conscious regarding the uniqueness of the perceptual scheme that unites members of this particular group into a homogeneous unit (the idea of a *heterogeneous* community being a contradiction in terms). Theological credos are consensus statements of common sentiments that bind members to each other and provide the structural form through which personal identity is crafted.

Communities, whatever their nature, are always repressive—though their repression may be *life-affirming* as well as potentially life-denying. The distinctive quality of religious communities in a pluralistic society is that one is free to choose the limiting structure through which one seeks liberation, purpose, and meaning. To reject the alternative of electing an historically conditioned community structure as the context for one's journey is to be left to one's personal resources in crafting a limiting principle or, alternatively, to wander through life with no definition of purpose.

The virtue of the Christian community as a context for identity construction is its wealth of symbolic forms. Thus, one enters a religious community which is replete with images, both ancient and modern, of what constitutes true existence. It is onto these symbolic forms that one imposes one's own history of experience, anticipating the imprint they will make as one strives for a centered self, a self which is reflective of the depth of one's religious heritage.

Religious educators are purveyors of tradition. Their task is to image the models which have been life-enabling in the past. And they have a more subtle task: to incorporate individuals into the life of the Christian community in order that they may be shaped by the symbolic forms (as well as the people) who comprise the community. It is the religious educators' task to make the weight of tradition a comfortable load—one which enables because it lights the way.

METHODS

Identity is structured within the Christian community on three levels: the *theoretical,* the *practical,* and the *sociological.* These are the three categories Joachim Wach, an early sociologist of religion, used to analyze religious community.[8] The *theoretical* level refers to the role of reason and intellect in the life of a community. Theologians sometimes assume this to be the exclusive concern of religion, which it is not, though the ideational side of religion is certainly important in that humans universally seek to define conceptually both themselves and their world. The *practical* level of religion is the dimension of worship and personal communion with the divine. It is often punctuated by ritual; rite and ritual being those time-honored forms that have enabled individuals to experience the deepest qualities of the human and the divine. The *sociological* level makes reference to the web of interpersonal relations which are often summarized in procedural norms of various types.

Religious educators err in attending to only one or another of these levels. To do so is to deny that humans are holistic beings, for each level serves a different aspect of our being. The theoretical serves the intellect; the ritualistic (or practical) serves the emotive; and the sociological relates to the communal. Identity is formed in an interpenetrating way on all of these levels. To focus on only the intellectual dimension is to exclude the emotive linkage which is so essential to the feeling of communal commitment. Likewise, an educational program that deals only with the social and the emotive excludes the role of reason in giving direction to the feelings.

Theoretical

The theoretical focus has been the traditional domain of religious education programs. Questions about curriculum usually refer to the content being taught. Older forms of religious education have involved children in learning catechisms and in memorizing Scripture. For adults, religious education has engaged men and women in Bible study, as well as in a study of doctrine. Often there has been a "right answer" to be learned (i.e., one which concurs with ecclesiastical authority).

Presently, because in many situations the theoretical dimension of Christianity is in dispute, religious education programs run the increasing possibility of having no assured content to teach. There is a positive aspect, however, to the present crisis in Christian theology: the fact that in many contexts theological propositions have as pronouncements lost their authority presents the subsequent opportunity for religious educators to explore the reasons specific doctrines or teachings have been important to the community. To recognize that theology is a human product— the human attempt to understand moral obligations in the face of a divine mystery which exceeds full human comprehension— invites individuals to contribute to the evolution of Christian theology through their own theological gropings. Surely theology and tradition become more real to individuals as their objectified status is demystified and as they have an occasion to further the reflective process.

With the demise in the last century of many of the most creative theological minds, we are left in a vacuum that encourages speculation on the nature of the divine. In this regard, the responsibility of the religious educator is to bring constantly to bear the tradition as a corrective to purely individualized flights of imagination; but creative exploration is appropriate. In spite of contemporary philosophy being decidedly antimetaphysical, the metaphysician in each of us yearns to define the Ultimate, and this is a process which religious education, at whatever level, may healthily encourage.

Practical

The practical element of religious education has been often ignored by Christian educators—especially Protestants.[9] Ritual has been conceived as belonging to worship, and worship services temporally have been separated from religious education in the eyes of many individuals. Such a hiatus is the unfortunate result of a failure to understand the important role ritual serves in forming identity. Ritual performs several distinct functions in identity formation. Emile Durkheim and such contemporaries as Victor Turner are perhaps our most articulate spokespersons on this point.[10] In Durkheim's view, it is in ritual that the symbols through which the community identifies itself are displayed. It is also in ritual that individuals often encounter a "presence" which is greater than the sum of those gathered for worship; perception of this presence is the bonding factor that unites individuals into one community. In addition, ritual performance carries with it a prescriptive order; to engage in ritual requires that one acknowledge the tradition which has made sacred certain objects and patterns of behavior.

Another use of ritual and rite in religious education is to formalize for the individual—and announce to the community—specific stages of religious development. Baptism, comfirmation, and, in the Jewish faith, Bar Mitzvah are three classic examples. Religious educators may profitably draw on these rites of passage as moments of identity confirmation in the religious life of individuals. Ritual is also a communal act of celebration. It is a moment when in a structured way the community addresses its center: the Presence referred to earlier. It is this experience of the sacred which grants legitimacy to the entire enterprise of religious education. Without the affective experience of ritual, the theoretical dimension of religion is sterile—mere abstract philosophy, not religion.

In the religious context, it is the affective quality of worship which provides the base for intellectual reflection. Theology is structured reflection on the divine-human encounter. Hence, religious education that proceeds without an experience of the sacred in worship is dead, comparable perhaps to the musicologist who only studies scores and never witnesses a live performance. Religious education cannot be the mere cataloging of others' experiences. To be meaningful it must be connected to an ongoing encounter with the wellsprings of communal life.

Sociological

The sociological dimension of religion refers to the intricate web of human associations which comprise community; it also is an important aspect of religious education. An individual feels committed to a particular way of life because of the affective bonds that link him or her with other individuals of similar persuasion. The community is a reference group, a body of significant others. The individual's identity is gained as it is mirrored in the response of others to his or her presence and participation in the community. The community tells that person who he or she is and what constitutes the limits of permissible behavior. Identity is always a product of social interaction, never the solitary ego contemplating itself.

It is within the community that the individual may probe and explore the limits of the Christian tradition and the flexibility of its symbolic expressions. Heresy within the community is safe; indeed, it is the very dynamic of change. Heresy only threatens the community when the one possessing a deviant voice moves outside the corporate discipline connoted by membership. Religious education proceeds on numerous nontangible levels, through informal discussions, conducting business, interacting with mentors, censuring deviants, and so on. Certainly as much is learned by doing as by studying or listening.

What should be obvious in this survey of the methods which undergird the educative function within a religious community is that the traditional teacher-pupil model of education is much too restrictive. Religious education embraces the whole experience of religious life within community. Consciousness is seldom transformed, identity seldom constructed, in the limited verbal exchange between pupil and teacher. Religious education is much more a matter of acculturation, with each formal period of instruction becoming a link in the chain of the larger process. Hence religious education occurs during worship and in the more mundane social interactions which occur within communal life, as well as in formalized instruction.

FUTURE

Religious education is not a narrowly defined task. In its broadest scope it teaches people how to live—and how to die. Its goal is to create whole people who have a self, a center, which makes the various facets (roles) of their lives meaningful ("ultimately" meaningful). First, the religious educator should teach independence of mind, so that no member of the Christian community is dependent upon success in any single role; community members should learn from their experience of the Christian faith that a more holistic reality embraces the particularity of any single failure. Second, religious educators should help grant to members of the Christian community what they most desire—a place to stand, a set of values that transpose and order the world. Third, religious educators in the Christian church should help prepare persons to engage in the journey of faith assured that there is a past from whence they have come and a meaningful future into which they may proceed.

Cultural pluralism threatens the religious enterprise, but only on the most superficial level. In fact, relativism opens up the question of truth in a fresh and pristine way. Old dogmas invite fresh reply; new pronouncements wait to be stated. The loss of traditional authority makes the pursuit of wisdom every person's opportunity. The breakdown of old forms is frequently followed by periods of religious ferment, with new theological and social forms being created. The relevance of religious institutions in an age of pluralism rests in their potential to forge identity. In a period when identity confusion is at a peak, the religious community, especially its liberal constituents, should not forsake the historic function of transforming individuals' lives.

In the final section of this book, I wish to move to a broader cultural perspective on the relevance of liberal Christianity to the modern age. In chapter 11 I offer a critique of the "therapeutic" mentality in modern society and suggest what I believe to be an appropriate response to this cultural shift. Chapter 12 deals with the worldwide phenomenon of secularization and offers a counterargument to the notion that religion is doomed in the long term. The final chapter examines what I believe to be one of the greatest threats faced by contemporary Christians: the increasing tendency to "explain away" religious experience and commitment through the use of sociological and psychological arguments. I offer in place of such reductionistic explanations some suggestions for a complementary relationship between theology and the social sciences.

NOTES

1. David Miller, *Gods and Games: Toward a Theology of Play* (New York: Harper & Row, 1970), and *The New Polytheism: Rebirth of the Gods and Goddesses* (New York: Harper & Row, 1974); also Harvey Cox, *Feast of Fools: A Theological Essay on Festivity and Fantasy* (New York: Harper & Row, 1969); *The Seduction of the Spirit: The Use and Misuse of People's Religion* (New York: Simon and Schuster, 1973).
2. Daniel Bell, "The Return of the Sacred? The Argument on the Future of Religion," *British Journal of Sociology* 28 (December 1977): 442.
3. Sigmund Freud, *Civilization and Its Discontents,* trans. and ed. James Strachey (New York: W. W. Norton, 1961), p. 42 ff.
4. For example, Bryan Wilson, *Contemporary Transformations of Religion* (Oxford: Oxford University Press, 1976); David Martin, *A General Theory of Secularization* Oxford: Basil Blackwell, 1978); Thomas Luckmann, *The Invisible Religion* (London: Collier-MacMillan, 1967); Peter Berger, *The Sacred Canopy: Elements of a Sociological Theory of Religion* (Garden City, N.Y.: Doubleday, 1967).
5. I am thinking here specifically of the writings of Francis Schaeffer, which have been influential within such groups as Inter-Varsity Christian Fellowship. For example, Francis Schaeffer, *The God Who Is There* (Downers Grove, Ill.: Inter-Varsity Press, 1966).
6. On the virtues of hypocrisy, see Bryan Wilson, *The Youth Culture and the Universities* (London: Faber, 1970), pp. 260–65.
7. See the excellent work by Hans Mol, *Identity and the Sacred* (Oxford: Basil Blackwell, 1976).
8. Joachim Wach, *The Sociology of Religion* (Chicago: University of Chicago Press, 1944).
9. One notable exception to this tendency is the work of John Westerhoff: for example, Gwen Kennedy Neville and John H. Westerhoff, III, *Learning Through Liturgy* (New York: Seabury Press, 1978).
10. Emile Durkheim, *The Elementary Forms of the Religious Life,* trans. Joseph Ward Swain (Glencoe, Ill.: Free Press, 1947); Victor Turner, *The Ritual Process: Structure and Anti-Structure* (Ithaca, N.Y.: Cornell University Press, 1969).

CHRISTIAN IDENTITY IN CONTEMPORARY SOCIETY

IV

A Critique of the
Therapeutic Mentality

11

AT THE turn of the century Max Weber wrote his famous *Protestant Ethic and the Spirit of Capitalism*, which to the present time has served as an important document of the life-style and values of the American people.[1] Although many have disputed the basic thesis of the work, few have attacked Weber's accuracy in describing the "ethic" and "spirit" of the time he was portraying. As an admirer of Weber's prodigious thought, I would not want to challenge his linkage between the "ethic" being "Protestant" and the "spirit" being "capitalism." I do find it interesting to speculate, however, on the title Weber might have given to his work if he had written it during the last decade.

My proposal is that today Weber, being the astute observer he was of cultural shifts, might have called his work *The Therapeutic Ethic and the Spirit of Tolerance.* This is not to suggest that capitalism is dead, nor even to suggest that few individuals still find their salvation in their work, but it is to argue that the dominant ethic of today has little to do with the strictures stereotypically identified with Puritanism. Rather, today's dominant ethic is much concerned with "doing your own thing," with self-development and self-fulfillment. And furthermore, the spirit of the day is one of tolerance toward the variety of forms in which individuals seek self-expression. It is in this cultural context that the liberal church functions.

Numerous attempts have been made to

describe the cultural shifts that have occurred in the last decade or so.[2] Most analyses focus on the 1960s as a time of political activism in which there was a concern with the justice of social institutions. In contrast, the seventies are portrayed as a time of turning inward, of exploring the realms of inner consciousness, expanding consciousness, and confronting elements of the self, which are repressed in the "journey outward."[3] Stated differently, the sixties were activistic, while the seventies were narcissistic. The eighties are yet to be defined.

Many commentators have argued that the failure in the sixties to make significant changes in the justice of social structures— to stop a war, to end poverty, etc.—produced a fatalistic attitude about the possibilities for changing a system that seemed to move under its own momentum, that seemed insensitive to external attempts at change. The consequence of this loss of confidence in changing the outside world was for people to turn inward, to work on a sphere that was more limited, more tangible, more amenable to manipulation. I am talking, of course, about the inner world of the psyche.

Americans being a pragmatic people who measure things by their success, I see numerous signs that the "myth of the therapeutic" for a significant number is showing signs of weakening. Peter Marin, writing in *Harper's,* called the spirit of the seventies "the new narcissism." Christopher Lasch followed, in the *New York Review of Books* and then in a major book, with the phrase "the narcissistic society." Tom Wolfe identified the seventies as "the 'Me' generation," and Karl Menninger was set to asking the question, "Whatever became of sin?"[4]

To write a requiem for the therapeutic would be presumptuous at this point—because that ethic, which has been at least a transient friend for many of us in the liberal church, is not yet dead. On the other hand, to prepare a funeral sermon that raises the question of "Where do we go from here?" has the advantage, perhaps, of hastening the death of the therapeutic by pointing to some alternatives which might exist beyond it.

DEFINING THE THERAPEUTIC ETHIC

But first, what is the therapeutic? I need to begin by making a disclaimer: by "the therapeutic" I am not referring to all forms of therapeutic intervention, particularly in the case of severely disturbed patients. Instead, I am referring to a mentality, an attitude, which pervades society particularly from the middle class and upward. It is a view that interprets reality in psychological and individualistic terms. Sheldon Wolin identified this mentality as "the rise of private man" and noted that it occurs "when the enterprise of psychology is inflated far beyond the requirements of a scientific inquiry and becomes the dominant mode of understanding, interpretation, and validation for both self and society."[5] Richard Sennett reversed Wolin's phrase in a book entitled *The Fall of Public Man.*[6] Whatever the therapeutic mentality is, it points to a rise in individualism and a decline in a commitment to community and goals which lie outside of the self.

The therapeutic ethic and its corresponding spirit of tolerance is represented in almost archetypical form in the "Gestalt prayer" penned some years ago by Fritz Perls, the early guru of many a proponent of the therapeutic.

> I do my thing, and you do your thing.
> I am not in this world to live up to your expectations
> And you are not in this world to live up to mine.
> You are you, and I am I,
> And if by chance, we find each other, it's beautiful.
> If not, it can't be helped.†

"I do my thing, and you do your thing" is perhaps the hallmark of the therapeutic ethic. Is there anything more "sacred" today, in terms of a moral norm, than the inviolable right to pursue one's own desires, wishes, intentions? The autonomy of moral conscience is surely one of the most agreed-upon social norms of the last decade.

"I am not in this world to live up to your expectations." The implicit assumption of this line is that other individuals do not exercise a claim over my individuality. If my interest is in maintaining my autonomy, then I will experience expectations of others as an intrusion on my private space. To deny the claims of others, of course, is to disclaim traditional notions of the moral responsibility of the individual to a community.

"You are not in this world to live up to [my expectations]"

† © Real People Press 1969. All rights reserved. Quoted from Frederick S. Perls, *Gestalt Therapy Verbatim* (New York: Bantam Books, 1971), frontispiece.

is a further rejection of the traditional norms of communal life. Community is founded upon the expectations which one individual has for another. From Perls' perspective, however, "You are you, and I am I, and if by chance we find each other, it's beautiful." The freedom of individualism and self-fulfillment is proclaimed eloquently in these two lines, which, of course, raise the question of what constitutes freedom. Is freedom the absence of constraint? Or, is one most free in the act of creative contributions to the social good?

Perls' last line, that if we do not find each other, well, "it can't be helped," expresses a note of fatalistic pessimism that symbolizes a distinct loss of contemporary social vision. It is an attitude of resignation to the fact that the world is not perfect and human beings do not always get along; consequently, "I'll at least try to get out of it for myself what I can." But another way of articulating this sentiment is to say that Perls has lost a vision of a better world, except as it might be defined in highly individualistic terms. Intentionally motivated social change always rests on a vision of what *could be*, not on the resignation implied by Perls' statement that "it can't be helped."

An aspect of the therapeutic not specifically mentioned in Perls' prayer is the emphasis upon getting in touch with one's own inner feelings. The thesis is that our socialization teaches us to cover over many of our "real" feelings in order to appear more polite, civilized, mature. In the process of repressing certain impulses and reactions, the individual loses touch with his or her spontaneity and "true" feelings and consequently ends up living a lie destructive to oneself. The therapeutic ethic counsels that it is good to get back in tune with primal feelings and experiences. Anger, joy, fear, repulsion, attraction should all be expressed directly in social interaction—so the therapeutic ethic encourages. The goal is to live a less repressed, more open, and aware existence.

The means for accomplishing this goal, of course, are numerous: weekend marathons, massage, rolfing, t'ai chi, nude encounters, assertiveness training, primal screaming, dance, and meditation are only a few of the techniques. The general point is that according to the therapeutic ethic we need to get in touch with our bodies and our emotions. We need to unlearn many of the values that living in community has taught us; the highest experiences are peak moments when the whole person is responding, pulsating, alive with energy, feeling.

The hallmark values of the therapeutic are self-fulfillment, self-actualization, authenticity, awareness. All these terms have individualistic connotations. Emotional well-being is viewed in purely personalistic ways; salvation is *personal* salvation. And how is satisfaction measured? In the moment. The therapeutic ethic is present-oriented, with a lack of concern for the future as well as often a disdain for the past—particularly in solving present emotional problems. In short, the therapeutic is generally ahistorical. It is what is happening in the present moment that is important.

HISTORICAL BACKGROUND

How are we to understand the high degree of individualism that is manifest currently among proponents of the therapeutic— not only at Esalen and during any number of group therapy sessions and marathon weekends, but also on a broader cultural level, including such pseudoreligions as *est*, many new religious movements, and so forth? Emile Durkheim, some eighty years ago, formulated an evolutionary view of social change which provides at least one perspective on current individualistic expressions of morality.

Durkheim argued that primitive societies, as a point of contrast with modern societies, are characterized by a form of mechanical solidarity in which persons resemble each other to a very high degree in terms of their moral and religious values. Social cohesion is based on the like-mindedness of persons with regard to beliefs and practice. Durkheim went as far as to state that mechanical solidarity is at its maximum *when personality is near the zero point.*[7] In contrast, modern societies are characterized by a high degree of structural differentiation, where because of the division of labor there is a variety of institutions, each performing different functions, allowing a corresponding opportunity for personal freedom, initiative, and innovation. The greater the division of labor, the greater shrinkage there is in the "collective conscience" and the more societies maintain social cohesion not on the basis of individuals' similarity, but on the basis of their interdependency.

According to Durkheim, one of the significant features of modern society is the emergence of "the cult of the individual."[8] Durkheim foresaw the decline of the traditional religious sphere, as measured by the authority of the priestly class and the strength of religious institutions, with a subsequent rise in the moral authority given over to the private sphere of the individual. Part of the pattern of secularization, according to Durkheim, is the gradual freeing of political, economic, and scientific functions from domination by the religious sphere; and part of this pattern of increasing autonomy is increased freedom in the personal sphere. Durkeim even described the individual as becoming "the object of a sort of religion."[9]

From Durkheim's perspective, then, the individualism to be found in the therapeutic ethic should come as no surprise. Also, increased tolerance of life-style diversity and idiosyncratic value is predictable with the institutional domain gradually giving more autonomy to individual desires for self-expression. Part of Durkheim's analysis, however, went beyond simply describing the direction of social evolution; he also expressed a genuine concern over the dangers endemic to the modern age. His analysis focused most specifically on the subject of suicide.[10] More generally, he was concerned with the anomic character of modern civilization in which individuals, because of their increased personal freedom unbounded by communal restrains, experience a loss of boundaries and norms. This state leads potentially to a state of anxiety and despondency.

MODERN INTERPRETATIONS

Many of Durkheim's concerns about modern society are given expression from a much different perspective in the writings of Philip Rieff, which further illuminate the nature of the therapeutic. In *The Triumph of the Therapeutic,* Rieff described a new character type that he saw emerging: "psychological man."[11] This character type follows in the wake of other historic character types, including "political man," "religious man," and "economic man."[12] Psychological man is the heir of psychoanalysis and Freud's pervasive cultural influence. This emergent character type is opposed to the restrictions imposed in all communal attachments. He takes himself as the ultimate project or center of value.

The unique characteristic of psychological man is that he uses the community for his own self-enhancement, but feels no ultimate commitment to any particular community. Rieff said that the change is from membership in "positive communities," which are based on commitment to the collectively held symbolic form, to "negative communities," which are based on information and social interchange, rather than the achievement of common communal goals.[13] Associating with others in negative communities, said Rieff, fits the desire of psychological man to be the *artist of his own life*, avoiding the constraints imposed when fulfillment is found in pursuing corporate goals. The therapeutic ethic is anti-doctrinal, anticreedal, nonprophetic. There is no law outside the individual; the self is the center of value.[14]

Psychological man is much more interested in being "pleased" than "saved," according to Rieff.[15] In an age of affluence, salvation is not the primary problem so much as is satiation and the need for entertainment. Psychological man is not worried about a unified world view as much as he is about living guiltlessly. The therapeutic ethic of tolerance is summarized in the statement: "Be kinder to the self!"[16] The character of contemporary culture, said Rieff, is one of "releases" triumphing over "controls." Indeed, some releases even sound like controls: e.g., "Be free!"[17] In summary, individuals are finding salvation increasingly in the amplitude of living itself, rather than in communal commitments.

In *The Triumph of the Therapeutic*, it was difficult for the reader to know whether Rieff was *for* the therapeutic or *against* it. In a later book, *Fellow Teachers*, this ambiguity was laid to rest.[18] He declared the therapeutic to be destructive of character, culture, and community. Operating from a psychoanalytic standpoint, Rieff identified character and culture with the restrictions and repressions imposed by living in community. Like Ernest Becker, he believed that "repression is truth," and he thereby held up a high place for what he called "interdicts."[19] He accosted modern education, which emphasizes experiences over learning the heritage of one's forefathers. Every genuine community must be creedal—meaning it must be interdictory.

To be radically contemporaneous, to be sprung loose from every particular symbolic, is to achieve a conclusive, unanswerable failure of historical memory. This is the uniquely modern achievement. Barbarians have never before existed. At the end of this tremendous cultural development, we moderns shall arrive at barbarism. Barbarians are people without historical memory. Barbarism is the real meaning of radical contemporaneity. Released from all authoritative pasts, we progress towards barbarism, not away from it.[20]

If Rieff was correct in his projection of a new character type of "psychological man," then I think the failure of the therapeutic lies in its inability to recognize the insight that true fulfillment, true humanity, is to be found in community, not in some autonomous, unbounded, unrepressed, ecstatic, primal, self-expressiveness. I am certainly not against such values held by the therapeutic as insight, maturity, and creativity. And, indeed, some individuals live insufferably repressed lives. So the foe is neither authority nor autonomy. The problem is achieving a balance between these two, a balance in which the demands of the community are checked by the need for personal integrity, and the drive for autonomous self-expression is countered by the demands of communal existence.

The failure of the therapeutic ethic is its narcissism. To make the ultimate goal self-fulfillment, getting in touch with feelings— self-realization—is to forget that one lives in community, in a world reliant upon interdependence. To turn inward, progressively unpeeling the layers of repression, is to arrive at the center only to find nothing—as when peeling an onion to its core. What gives an individual a center, from my perspective, is his or her rootedness in a community, in the collective purposes that bind a group of people together. Fulfillment is to be achieved through one's contribution to the life of the community. This achievement may be artistic, creative, and have overtones of appearing individualistic; and yet the measure of the product is the degree to which it contributes to the enhancement of the collective body. The fullness of experience is to participate in the web of life that includes a sense of continuity with those who have come before, those who will follow, and those in the present to whom one owes one's life.

I suspect that one of the underlying reasons for the emphasis of the therapeutic ethic on living in the present is the fear shared by all of us that there may be no tomorrow.[21] The threat of nuclear war, the awareness that natural resources are running out—these are two situations that previous generations have not faced simultaneously. I sense in myself a certain pessimism about the future which affects the way I feel about such activities as working for long-range social changes and building physical structures that will last generations. And yet, in spite of the threat of a futureless tomorrow, it strikes me as imperative that we set about constructing the New Jerusalem or its equivalent. Without a collective vision there is only despair once the ecstasy of the moment has worn off.

Freud's wayward disciple, Alfred Adler, offered a perspective in his principle of "social interest" that poses a helpful qualification to the individualism of the therapeutic.[22] Adler argued that the source of all neurosis, psychosis, and criminality is the failure of individuals to develop a sense of collective responsibility.[23] By social interest, Adler was referring to a sense of "fellow feeling" in which individuals possess a realization of both their dependence on others and their responsibility for others. Adler often told his patients: "You can be cured in fourteen days if you follow this prescription. Try to think every day how you can please someone."[24] Admittedly, this prescription is somewhat simplistic, but on another level the insight is profound. It gives witness to the brotherhood and sisterhood of humankind, a situation in which from childhood we are dependent and helpless, gaining strength from our relationships with others.

The failure of the therapeutic ethic is in the counsel that salvation is to be found in living for oneself. I suspect that much of the free-floating anxiety that presently characterizes individuals is due to the repressed guilt associated with a socially irresponsible life-style. According to Adler, emotional health is to be found in caring for the disenfranchised of our society: the poor, the elderly, the physically and mentally unfit. These are the activities that contribute to fulfillment in life. Getting in touch with one's body, feelings, and emotions is to be saluted only so long as this activity contributes to and does not preclude demonstrable social involvement.

To be part of a genuine community is to live under the authority of the symbolic structures that give purpose and meaning to the members of the community. Discipline, demands, strictures—these are all positive aspects of being bound to other individuals in relationships which bring mutual fulfillment. Service to the community is not a denial of the self, but the fulfillment of the self. It is in this context that I see the functional role of guilt as a signal of social transgressions.[25] Admittedly, guilt can be neurotic and immensely destructive. On the other hand, it is the community that has the power to forgive transgressions, and without the sensitivity of conscience it is all too easy to imagine that we are our own makers, independent, self-sufficient, and owing no one for our existence.

A NEW TRIBALISM

What would be a productive step beyond the therapeutic ethic to a mode of existence that recognizes both the virtues of this ethic and yet seeks a modification of it along the lines of greater social responsibility? I wish to propose an image of social transformation that might be described as a "new tribalism." It would not be a tribalism in which group is pitted against group, nor would it be a situation in which the tribe would smother the individuality of its members. Rather, the new tribalism would be a social system based on an increasing number of intimate communities in which individuals could experience the warmth of a small group and yet at the same time be part of a group that could be a significant political force. I am less clear on what these communities would look like than I am as to their necessity. Undoubtedly the nuclear family is too small and too homogeneous to service properly the individual in the broad range of his or her physical, emotional, and spiritual needs, although the extended family might fulfill some of these needs. My own choice would be for the church, or the religious community, to function as the tribal unit that one would join. And yet I am aware of the resistance of many individuals to religious institutions. Durkheim thought that labor unions or guilds might provide a communal center for individuals.

Whatever the functional unit would be, it should include some of the following features:

(1) Individuals would be bound together by commonly shared goals and purposes that would be democratically instituted and maintained.

(2) Individuals would freely submit to the discipline of living under the authority of community.

(3) The community would be a place where one would care for the needs of others in the group and feel confident that one's own needs would be cared for.

(4) Children would be nurtured as well as the elderly.

(5) In spite of the particularism of one's commitment to a specific community, a sense of solidarity with the needs and future of the whole human community would be emphasized.

(6) Each community would respect cultural diversity—meaning other tribal units would not need to resemble one's own.

(7) An individual would be free at any time to leave the community. Also, constructive criticism of the community would be encouraged and tolerated.

Following Durkheim, a community that fits these requirements would need to take on some of the expressions traditional to religious communities. More specifically, Durkheim argued for the importance of rite and ritual in binding a community together. Individuals, he argued, need regular ways in which they can rehearse the collective sentiments that unite them. Rituals aid in celebrating the common values which members of the community share as well as recalling and dramatizing the events which are important to the community's history. It seems to me that the above seven points, when related to Durkheim's theory, are descriptive of the liberal church. Furthermore, I would suggest that to the extent that the liberal church is one expression of the new tribalism—which I am proposing it is—its members should renew their appreciation and use of the role of ritual in building community.

The *self-conscious* practice of ritual may seem incongruous with our traditional notions of ritual as imbued by a sacred power. Yet in recent years I see numerous instances of individuals participating in religious rituals and being not so concerned with the literal character of their theological content so much as they are with the importance of ritual as an instrument of communal self-transformation (within which the sacred is manifest). Most poignant in my memory is the case of a Jewish student who was raised in a very secular home and then at age twenty-five joined a Hillel group in which collectively, with a group of other secular Jewish students, she weekly celebrated all of the traditional rites of the Jewish community. She did not profess to understand all the theological trappings of what she was doing, but she was able to appreciate the feeling such participation gave to her of being tied to a tradition, a community where people shared the same values and mentality. Also noteworthy is that what began as something of a psycho-social experiment turned into a very definite theological commitment and understanding. In my own Episcopal church there are a number of people who are not at all certain what the creeds mean if taken literally, and yet that does not preclude them from regularly reciting the creeds or from participating in Holy Communion, the central sacrament of the church. As argued previously, I honor such participation because it is through the experience of contacting on a regular basis the symbolic forms of the Christian church that faith may be kindled.

Why do these individuals find ritual observance to be an important part of their experience? Emile Durkheim observed that it is through ritual that individuals become conscious of their corporate identity. Ritual observance provides the occasion for the experience of the feeling that there is something greater than the mere aggregate presence of those gathered together. In my image of the new tribalism, groups would be self-conscious about the need for corporate rituals and would devote considerable energies to their creation. The church, of course, begins with a considerable advantage over purely secular groups because of its rich heritage of symbolic enactment.

Finally, a word of explanation is due if what I am proposing in the way of the new tribalism sounds all too much like another therapy group. Herein lies my ambivalence: the therapy group is not intrinsically bad in terms of counseling the values of openness and directness. What is wrong with the therapeutic mentality is that it is *incomplete*. It fails too often to acknowledge the need that individuals have for a purpose which transcends themselves. It is not enough for a group of people to gather for the purpose of seeking self-help, as exemplified in the marathon weekend or the weekly therapy group. That will never lead to fulfillment. An important aspect of personal meaning is in attachment to a larger collective purpose. The failure of group therapy to achieve a lasting impact on individuals is due to the fact that once the therapy group dissolves, the individual is again cast back into a situation that in many instances lacks close communal affiliation.

If the new tribalism is successfully executed, the therapeutic function would be incorporated into the life of the community. Many features of group therapy have their religious correlate (e.g. confession, absolution, etc.). Thus, even though the tribal unit might not necessarily be religious in any traditional sense, the religious community would be potentially in a preeminent place to service the therapeutic needs of its members.

In conclusion, let me stress that the argument I am making is not an indictment of psychotherapy per se, but of the therapeutic as a culturally pervasive mentality. I see a legitimate role for psychotherapists in helping individuals to experience the fullness of life. My concern is that full existence be defined in terms of one's social and moral responsibility to communal life. Finally, it should be evident that, from my view, the religious institution (i.e., the church) is the social group with the longest tradition of dealing with the diverse needs of the human psyche while still directing its members to concerns that supersede the needs of group members. Many individuals currently are joining religious organizations for primarily therapeutic reasons. Obviously, this form of tribalism misses the mark in my estimation. On the other hand, there are religious institutions which, in the process of ministering to the emotional and physical needs of their members, act as significant agents of social change as they unite their community around the bonds of a common symbolic form.

NOTES

1. Max Weber, *The Protestant Ethic and the Spirit of Capitalism*, trans. Talcott Parsons (New York: Charles Scribner's Sons, 1958).
2. One of the best recent collections of essays on this subject is Herbert J. Gans et al., eds., *On the Making of Americans: Essays in Honor of David Riesman* (Philadelphia: University of Pennsylvania Press, 1979).

3. Harvey Cox, *Turning East: The Promise and Peril of the New Orientalism* (New York: Simon & Schuster, 1977).

4. Peter Marin, "The New Narcissism," *Harper's Magazine*, October 1975, pp. 45–56; Christopher Lasch, "The Narcissistic Society," *The New York Review of Books*, September 30, 1976, p. 5 ff.; Karl Menninger, *Whatever Became of Sin?* (New York: Hawthorn Books, 1973); Tom Wolfe, "The 'Me' Decade and the Third Great Awakening," *New York*, August 23, 1976, pp. 26–40.

5. Sheldon Wolin, "The Rise of Private Man," *The New York Review of Books*, April 14, 1977, p. 19 ff.

6. Richard Sennett, *The Fall of Public Man* (New York: Knopf, 1976).

7. Emile Durkheim, *The Division of Labor in Society*, trans. George Simpson (New York: Free Press, 1960), p. 130.

8. Ibid.

9. Ibid., pp. 172–73.

10. Emile Durkheim, *Suicide: A Study in Sociology* (New York: Free Press, 1954).

11. Philip Rieff, *The Triumph of the Therapeutic: Uses of Faith After Freud* (New York: Harper & Row, 1966), pp. 34–41.

12. Philip Rieff, *Freud: The Mind of a Moralist* (Garden City, N.Y.: Doubleday, Anchor Books, 1961), p. 391.

13. Rieff, *Triumph of the Therapeutic*, pp. 52–53.

14. Ibid., pp. 60–62.

15. Ibid., pp. 24–5.

16. Ibid., p. 58.

17. Ibid., pp. 233–39.

18. Philip Rieff, *Fellow Teachers* (New York: Harper & Row, 1973).

19. Philip Rieff, "The Impossible Culture: Wilde as a Modern Prophet," in *The Soul of Man Under Socialism*, by Oscar Wilde (New York: Harper & Row, 1970), p. xvi.

20. Rieff, *Fellow Teachers*, p. 39.

21. Robert Jay Lifton, *Boundaries: Psychological Man in Revolution* (New York: Random House, Vintage Books, 1970), pp. 21–36.

22. Alfred Adler, *Social Interest: A Challenge to Mankind* (New York: Capricorn, 1964).

23. Alfred Adler, *What Life Should Mean to You* (New York: Capricorn, 1958), p. 8.

24. Ibid., p. 259.

25. See Roger W. Smith, ed., *Guilt: Man and Society* (Garden City, N.Y.: Doubleday, Anchor Books, 1971).

Secularization and the Liberal Prospect

12

THE RELIGIOUS enterprise is in many quarters assessed as being of antiquarian interest only. For these "modern" individuals there is no denial of religion's place in the past, but they conceive of themselves as having outgrown such obsessive behavior. Religion is something for primitives and for those who need a supernatural helper to cope with life's travails. They, however, have graduated to a new level of sophistication, both in analyzing natural and human problems and in ameliorating them. True, they may occasionally go to church. But church-going is more of a leisure time activity than anything else. The church is a place of sociability, of moral instruction, and occasionally of enlightening lectures on various social and personal ills. But religion is perceived to have little personal relevance, except perhaps to punctuate the transitions of the life cycle: birth, marriage, death.

Many professional commentators note these trends in religious consciousness and observe that religion is on the ebb, except perhaps among certain "socially regressive" groups.[1] In their view, the future surely is religionless. Considerable evidence is sometimes cited. The low church attendance in western Europe (the United States is a strange anomaly), the lower percentages of attendance among the young than among the middle aged and elderly, the lessening influence of the church in political affairs, and so forth.[2] In short, *religious change* is interpreted as *religious demise.* Usually some type of evolutionary model of human development is summoned in defense of these conjectures (i.e., we are becoming progressively more rational).

On a somewhat more philosophical level, the demise of religion is often correlated with new insights into the nature of language (especially myth and symbol), and the social conditionedness of all knowledge, and the various difficulties in harmonizing a scientific world view with a first century biblical cosmology. Religion, in this vein, is interesting as a subject for study, but not for commitment. Religious studies courses one observes are popular on the university campus. The study of religion in this context, however, is often synonymous with debunking—discovering the misconceptions of childhood religion—or else the survey of competing meaning systems (which is a relativizing activity).

THE NATURE OF HUMANITY

The thesis of this chapter is that changes both in existing religious institutions and in patterns of traditional commitment are not necessarily synonymous with the demise of religion. I think a more accurate perception of religious change is one that views such alterations as the creative evolution of the human spirit in search of a reason for being. This thesis stands on the assumption that human beings are essentially religious animals: that what distinguishes them from the "beasts" is that they inquire into the meaning of life, the purpose of their being. According to this assumption, it is not sufficient just to work and procreate. Individuals also seek to know what is the meaning of their work, what is really worthwhile, what is truly of significance. Individuals wish to know that their lives count for something beyond the triviality of disconnected role performances.

In my view it is mistaken to interpret the survival of existing institutional forms as synonymous with the preservation of religion, although I suspect that a hundred years from now there will be more Baptists, Presbyterians, Episcopalians, and Catholics around than many secular commentators suspect. Also, in my view, institutional religion is not going to give way to an exclusively personalized religion. Man's search for meaning inevitably takes social form—this in spite of an increasingly individualistic culture.[3] Some would suggest that in spite of the preservation of religion in some quarters, the quest for ultimate values and ultimate frames of reference is at an end. Personally, I have difficulty believing that the current evasion of ultimate questions is anything more than a temporary myopia caused by a philosophically unsophisticated infatuation with scientism. This myopia, I believe, should be interpreted as a transitory denial of meaning and not as an affirmation of what is essentially human. The failure to define life within some framework of values—ethical prescriptions inevitably calling out for some metaphysical reference—is an aberration of the human: a state not to be applauded, but to be decried, for it means that human beings are giving up the very best in themselves, that which defines their humanity as valuing, purpose-seeking beings.

Theologians have expressed variously this fundamental human quality to seek meaning. Augustine stated in his *Confessions* that "Man's heart is restless until it rests in thee."[4] Tillich, in somewhat more contemporary language, defined the religious search as the "quest for being."[5] Indeed, some existentialist writers have evidenced their fundamental humanity by proclaiming "meaninglessness" to be the Ultimate that is at the heart of the universe.[6] But to decry this fact, as did Nietzsche and others, is to show one's fundamentally human concern with the issue of meaning. To be religious does not mean that one has found an answer; it implies rather that one is on a truth quest. In fact, the more vehement one's protest against the possibility of metaphysics, the more ultimately one shows himself or herself to be on a quest for ultimate meaning.

The religious quest may not be expressed verbally; it may be much more behaviorally defined: as in frenzied sensuality, frenetic work patterns, or fanatical political commitments. It is ambiguous whether such activities are the affirmation of an ultimate value or the nonconscious attempt to deny a feeling of vacuity. Dread, anxiety, the empty feeling that may fill one's consciousness upon awakening—these are all correlates of the human urge for meaning and purpose. Not to feel the threat of meaninglessness is to be half dead or, perhaps more appropriately, only half human.

DEFINING RELIGION

It is in the face of this definition of humanity that I speak of the eternal verity of religion. But to speak of religion requires further clarification of the definition of the term. Religion has been defined both *functionally* and *substantively*.[7] *Functional definitions* argue that religion exists because it helps individuals to cope with the ultimate threats of existence: death, suffering, and the uncontrollable vicissitudes of the natural world.[8] Also, religion is often seen to function as the legitimating force underlying personal values and social norms. The claim is made by functionalist interpreters that religion will not disappear until there is no more human suffering, no more death, and no more need to be shielded from the terrors of existence. Also, the claim is made that the human community is ungovernable without the divine sanction of the sacred in justifying certain civilizing conventions.[9]

Substantive definitions, in contrast, focus on specific religious feelings and experiences obtained by individuals at definable moments in time and space. Religion is said to be concerned with an encounter with/by the Holy.[10] Feelings of awe, reverence, humility are often cited as qualities of religious experience. Religious experience may be coincident with the feeling of being incorporated into the whole fellowship of being, or participating in the oneness of all things. The feelings of unity, interconnectedness, and integration are often cited as aspects of religious experience. The symbol of God may emerge in these descriptions; most certainly the language of ultimacy is used.

To my mind, however, one need not choose between functional and substantive definitions. Undoubtedly both are appropriate on some level. Religion indeed exists because it functions to fulfill certain human needs; and there is necessarily also a substantive quality to the quest for being. So I see little purpose in throwing one more definition into the welter of existing pronouncements. I do wish, however, to suggest that an adequate definition of religion must take into account three human proclivities, each of which points to the survival power of religion: (1) the need to *commit* oneself to something greater than oneself; (2) the need to find *release* from one's own failure to live up to certain self-imposed standards, and (3) the need for *interconnectedness* on a social and cosmic plane.

The Need for Commitment

Existence that revolves totally around one's own personal requirements is finally experienced as empty and meaningless. This need to be committed to something greater than oneself is productive of attachments to a variety of causes—both for good and for ill. In such commitments, the individual seeks identification with projects that mitigate his or her own mortality and link him or her to the essential structures of existence. Whether the cause is the creation of a pure race, the elimination of all who fail to embrace the truth, or the struggle to bring justice and equality to all humankind, commitment to a philosophy (and often to a person as the purveyor of that point of view) may be the source of meaning and purpose in existence. One who has no commitments lives in the moment, unrooted by the constraints which abide through the act of giving oneself to some idea or to someone.

To take one's own fulfillment as an end in itself, unattached to any wider sphere of social responsibility, is to express the pathological state of narcissism. As was noted in a previous chapter, Alfred Adler made central to his model of healthy existence what he called "social interest." Individuals who take themselves as their only projects in life are, in Adler's view, neurotic and unhappy. Meaning and purpose, in his opinion, require engagement in the act of caring for others, involvement in the larger sphere of the human enterprise. Sustained narcissism finally leads to bitterness and isolation. The act of commitment, in contrast, expands the individual, opening him or her to the joy of feeling tied to a larger purpose. The life-enhancing character of commitment reaches its apex in those choices which lead to ultimate commitment and therefore to metaphysical meaning.

The Need for Release

In the search for meaning, individuals set standards for themselves. These are standards of conduct and attitude governing how they should relate to others as well as to themselves. The standards may be cosmically grounded or they may be much more individualistic. Nevertheless, they are self-imposed rules whose transgression produces guilt and anxiety. Freud, the master liberator, reminds us, however, that no society can function without cultural interdicts.[11] Constraint is essential to community. Nevertheless, the human drive for self-assertion and dominance continually involves individuals in violating corporately legislated rules. Theologically this experience of transgression has been classically defined as "sin." Culturally and philosophically, it has been viewed as moral failure.

Release from guilt is essential to healthy, joyful existence. Religious communities have recognized this need by inculcating rites of confession, sacrifice, oblation. "Catharsis" is the word used for the "confessions" that transpire between psychiatrist and patient. The parallels between the therapeutic and priestly roles are undeniable.[12] Self-punishment (masochism) is the consequence of moral failure which is not ameliorated in some more symbolic way. Life that is not cleansed on some level is fettered with too many burdens to allow one to live a life of creative, joy-filled involvement.

The Need for Connectedness

Humans are by nature gregarious; they are also philosophical. Interconnectedness is sought on a social as well as on a cosmic plane. Loneliness is the emergent curse of an urban, impersonal society; anomie is the consequence of a broader social failure to inspire experiences of mutuality and communalization. Suicide is the not infrequent result when an individual feels that he or she does not matter, that there is nothing to live for, that he or she is unimportant to the community. "Psychic despair" is the more abstract expression of feeling unwanted on a cosmic plane. The death of God was greeted in few quarters with celebration, for human beings desire to be metaphysically rooted, their lives participating in a divine order which transcends the plane of chance and happenstance.

The strength of religion, if it has no other (even in its more fanatical forms), is that it allows individuals to feel they are needed, loved, and essential to the larger communal purpose. Critics have faulted religion for being too much of a *social* enterprise, but such criticism evidences a failure to understand the human need for interconnectedness. Personal identity is bred in community, and the feeling of being connected to the cosmos in some meaningful way is often gained through participation in a community that one feels, on some level, is a microcosmic reflection of a larger Ultimate order. Hence, in community both interpersonal and transhistorical interconnections may be realized. For some, interconnectedness is sought divorced from community: individuals seek ultimate union through meditative exercises, privations of various sorts, as well as through the opposite state: total indulgence in the fullness of human experience—sexual, mental, physical.

SECULARIZING FORCES

One reason for the *apparent* demise of religion in some quarters is that each of the three rules which religion has traditionally serviced—*commitment, release, interconnectedness*—has been, to some degree, usurped by nonreligious forces. *The human need to be committed* to certain ideals has been replaced by the seductive power of consumerism. In affluence, in the accumulation of goods, in the intoxication of buying, people have temporarily lost sight of their need for ideals/commitments. The quest for meaning has become the quest for things. The "restless heart" of St. Augustine now seeks security in the material world. Anxieties over the proper end of life have been replaced by the simplistic maxim: more is better.

The need for release from the burdens of living is being serviced in the contemporary situation by two sources: pharmaceutical prophylactics and the psychotheraphy industry. Release from guilt is achieved (masked?) by steady doses of Valium and Librium. Release from the pain of defiled relationships is accomplished through the instrumentality of the therapist who says, "You are too hard on yourself." Lower standards, a more permissive ethic, fewer interdicts is the solution to a guilty conscience. Who needs mechanisms for forgiveness if there is no way to sin?

The need for interconnectedness is being served for many individuals (four to five hours a day) by the artificial connection they have with others through the medium of television. I do not think we can underestimate the way television is altering contemporary culture. For one thing, television occupies the time individuals might otherwise use relating to family and friends. Individuals do not need to learn the fine art of conversation or to engage in communal forms of sociability when their attention can be saturated with "entertainment." The imagination formerly invested in building community is drained into solving television murder plots or anticipating answers on quiz shows. Engagement with one's own family is usurped by the vicarious experience of watching problems solved in *All in the Family*. Marriages dissolve, children feel alienated from parents. Why? Because, in part, individuals have not developed the skills to communicate with each other.

THE FUTURE OF RELIGION

In terms of the issue being considered in this chapter—the future of religion—the question is whether the needs for commitment, release, and interconnectedness will in the long term be as adequately served by the profane substitutes just mentioned as they were formerly served by their religious alternatives. To answer such a question would require the powers of a seer. Lacking any prophetic abilities, the most I can hope to do in concluding this chapter is clarify two alternatives that I foresee as possibilities, arguing for the worthwhileness of the second alternative. The first scenario, to which I will only allude, is an extension of consumerism, drugs/psychotherapy, and television saturation. Concurrent with this scenario are increasingly rationalized institutions, declining community, greater bureaucracy, and a mindless narcissism. Max Weber has adequately described this alternative in his statement at the end of *The Protestant Ethic and the Spirit of Capitalism*.

> Fate decreed that the cloak [of capitalism and machine production] should become an iron cage. . . . For of the last stage of this cultural development, it might well be truly said: "Specialists without spirit, sensualists without heart; this nullity imagines that it has attained a level of civilization never before achieved."[13]

On the other hand, I believe it is possible to present a more optimistic alternative to Weber's description of the modern age. First, there are already signs that the affluence of American culture may have reached its zenith and entered a period of long-term regression. The oil crisis may be the mere tip of the iceberg. And as inflation continues to erode buying power, it is possible that consumerism may not only lose its hypnotic charm, but may become a nonviable option. Personally, I have little doubt but that we can anticipate a less consumptive future: the world's resources simply cannot sustain the current level of depletion. At first glance this may seem disastrous—but that is only because we have come to measure the quality of life in terms of its quantity. I strongly suspect that when increasing numbers of people in the Western world can no longer afford to make the quantity = quality equation, then we will see a rebirth of idealism and a new search for causes and programs that are worthy of our commitment.[14]

The future of the other two areas, *release* mechanisms and the need for *interconnectedness,* is less easy to prognosticate. But I do see some flags in the wind. As mentioned in chapter 11, the likes of Christopher Lasch, Philip Rieff, Tom Wolfe, Peter Marin, and others have been offering prophetic utterances that increasingly seem to be attracting attention and that militate against the decadence of the "therapeutic mentality." The immediate zest derived from pursuing one's own self-interest may prove unable to withstand the test of time. Liberation to impulsive behavior is not identical with liberation of the self. Indeed, liberation is of little avail unless one can be liberated *for* something—which reintroduces the role of values and commitment to ultimate meaning systems. Rieff may have been right when he implied that truth resides in repression, for only by *standing against* some things can one *stand for* anything. And pharmaceutical aids "cure" nothing. They merely offer temporary relief, release, or help stabilize thought processes; they contain no directive to happiness or fulfillment.

I feel less certain about predicting the demise of television. It is such an easy entertainment that to predict its lessening influence calls for a statement about human nature. Will people have the strength of character to place in proper perspective this "gift" of technology? I don't know. But those who are strong of character will do so, and perhaps that is enough to initiate the revolt. Also, and in this I place more stock, if the chain of affluence is broken, then I believe we can expect profound changes in the rest of our social life, including television-viewing—for after all, it is commercials that support "the tube." Furthermore, I have faith that there are few satisfactions better than those derived from communal engagements and nonsuperficial conversation and that eventually we will see a return to person-to-person exchanges, as opposed to person-to-mechanized technology exchanges.

To argue the reversals I have suggested in these three areas flies in the face of several long-term trends that offer serious challenges to the scenario for which I have argued. The world is becoming more and more rationalized (in the Weberian sense of that term).[15] Instrumental thinking, in which "means" dominate or justify "ends," increasingly predominates. A pseudoscientific rationalism is, on a popular level, progressively neutralizing discussion of moral absolutes and philosophical ultimates. There is little legitimacy in the modern age for the poetic, the nonrational, and the noninstrumental.

The long-term trend seems to be away from community and towards a societal individualism. Ferdinand Tönnies heralded the day of a faceless suburbia and alienated urban populations in his description of the historical progression from *Gemeinschaft* to *Gesellschaft* forms of social organization. Presently, voluntary associations are increasingly patronized by individuals on the basis of the benefits they can derive from these groups, as opposed to an older pattern in which individuals served communal ideals because of their commitment to corporate goals. Often the truest forms of community in the urban core are those that have formed around illicit activities, which is a sad commentary on contemporary institutional life.

In spite of the apparent dreariness of the human prospect, at the most basic level—and I suppose it is a matter of faith—I believe that individuals will not allow their humaneness to be extinguished. They will assert the importance of the quest for wholeness through their commitment to ideals and in their search for moral absolutes. They will conclude that the only *final* release is one which is based upon metaphysical absolution for the sin of failing to live up to, not self-imposed moral standards, but universal moral standards rooted in the very nature of things. People will tire of their isolation and of the individualism that has surfaced in response to a consumer oriented society in which "your gain is my loss."

THE TASK OF THE LIBERAL CHURCH

The liberal church has the opportunity to be a guiding light to the society as a whole—if it can walk the tightrope of being open to the culture around it while remaining true to the insight that man is not sufficient unto himself. The Christian church should ideally be the place where individuals may search for ultimates and discover values to which they may commit themselves. The symbolic form of Jesus is not bound by time. Men and women in all ages can be seized by the example of Christ's selflessness, his ministry to the poor and needy, his proclamation of love, his relationship to a power that transcended himself. This is the vision, while subject to reinterpretation in every cultural and historical setting, which is nevertheless timeless. As for the symbolic forms which the church evolved, those through which individuals have found forgiveness, strength, vision, and a sense of communion with a power beyond them and with those around them—one wonders if they will not also continue. Only doctrine, frozen in dogmatism, will not survive the march of time.

NOTES

1. See, for example, Bryan Wilson, *Religion in Secular Society* (London: Watts, 1966), and *Contemporary Transformations of Religion* (Oxford: Oxford University Press, 1976).
2. There is a wide variety of works on secularization; for example, Peter Berger, *The Sacred Canopy: Elements of a Sociological Theory of Religion* (Garden City, N.Y.: Doubleday, 1967), Part II; David Martin, *A General Theory of Secularization* (Oxford: Basil Blackwell, 1978); *The Dilemmas of Contemporary Religion* (Oxford: Basil Blackwell, 1978); James F. Childress and David Harned, eds., *Secularization and the Protestant Prospect* (Philadelphia: Westminster Press, 1970).
3. Thomas Luckmann, *The Invisible Religion* (London: Macmillan, 1967).

4. St. Augustine, *The Confessions of St. Augustine,* trans. Edward Pusey (London: Collier-Macmillan, 1961).

5. Paul Tillich, *The Courage to Be* (New Haven, Conn.: Yale University Press, 1952), esp. pp. 155–190.

6. Albert Camus, *The Stranger,* trans. Stewart Gilbert (New York: Random House, Vintage Books, 1946), p. 154.

7. Peter Berger, "Some Second Thoughts on Substantive Versus Functional Definitions of Religion," *Journal for the Scientific Study of Religion* 13, no. 2 (June 1974): 125–133.

8. J. Milton Yinger, *Religion, Society and the Individual* (New York: Macmillan, 1957), pp. 7–12.

9. For other functional approaches to religion, see Elizabeth Nottingham, *Religion: A Sociological View* (New York: Random House, 1971); Thomas O'Dea, *The Sociology of Religion* (Englewood Cliffs, N.J.: Prentice-Hall, 1966).

10. Rudolf Otto, *The Idea of the Holy,* trans. J. W. Harvey (Oxford: Oxford University Press, 1928).

11. Philip Rieff, *Freud: The Mind of a Moralist* (Garden City, N.Y.: Doubleday, Anchor Books, 1961).

12. Thomas Oden, *The Intensive Group Experience: The New Pietism* (Philadelphia: Westminster, 1972).

13. Max Weber, *The Protestant Ethic and the Spirit of Capitalism,* trans. Talcott Parsons (New York: Charles Scribner's Sons, 1958), pp. 181–82.

14. See my article on inflation: Donald E. Miller, "Resurrecting Disaster: Reflections on Inflation," *The Christian Century,* September 12, 1979, pp. 869–70.

15. On rationalization, bureaucratization, and routinization, see Max Weber, *From Max Weber: Essays in Sociology,* ed. and trans. (with intro. by) H. H. Gerth and C. Wright Mills (New York: Oxford University Press, 1958), esp. pp. 196–244.

Theology and the
Social Sciences

13

I BELIEVE that the greatest challenge to personal religious commitment in the last half-century has been not from the physical or biological sciences, nor even from the field of philosophy, but from the social sciences. The question of the *truth* of religion has subtly been subsumed under the headings: How does religion *work?* What are its social and psychological *functions?*

On the face of many psychological or sociological analyses the truth claims of religion are not attacked. It is by innuendo and inference that religious truth claims are called into question: namely, that if one can explain how religion *works,* then one has explained religion *away.* The debunking of religion may be explicit—as in the case of commentators such as Emile Durkheim, who believed that he had identified society as the "true" object of religious devotion. Or the threat to religious truth claims may be more implicit, as in the case of Max Weber, where a sociological interpretation is offered of how religions emerge and evolve.

Why is it that many people with personal religious commitments feel threatened when the social-psychological dynamics of the religious life are analyzed? I suspect that it is because they fear the analyst believes there is *nothing more* to these experiences than the human element. In many instances their fear is probably justified. On the other hand, to be too threatened by the metaphysical conclusions of those investigating how religion works is to ignore the validity of these investigators' descriptive insights in order to focus on their nonempirical, largely unself-conscious philosophical assumptions. In some curious way, the assumptions of these investigators gain facticity (truth value) as a result of being paired with their empirical observations.

The fear that many religionists feel towards sociological and psychological explanation seems to me, however, to be altogether groundless. I wish to show in this chapter why I hold this position, and in addition I will attempt to specify the conditions under which theologians and social scientists might engage in fruitful conversation.

SOME INCORRECT ASSUMPTIONS

The tension between theology and the social sciences rests, I believe, on two factors. First, many sociologists, psychologists, and anthropologists subtly intertwine their descriptions of religious experience with their pronouncements about the truth of religion. Logically, description and prescription are separable, since there is no purely rational leap one can make from one to another without inserting an intervening value assumption.[1] Nevertheless, the personal pronouncements of someone such as Freud gain authority by virtue of their association with his case descriptions. At this point, I wish simply to state that the connection is not automatic between the way a religion works and the truth value it carries. Even a pragmatic measure of truth rests on the assertion of *a priori* assumptions.

Second, to assume that religious experience does not have its social-psychological correlates seems to me to rest on an untenable notion of truth. Truth, in its most absolute sense, may indeed exist independent from human embodiment—in that sense, truth is pristine, pure, unadulterated. Nevertheless, to the extent that human beings appropriate that truth—conceptualize it, theorize about it, embody it in doctrine, creed, and ritual—it becomes tainted by human form, and necessarily so! Human beings inevitably bring to their search for truth a background of experiences that predispose them toward particular expressions of religion; furthermore, the way in which they speak of ultimate things reflects the culture in which they live, its language, the limitations of the world view in which they have been acculturated, and so on. Human beings are limited in their powers of conceptualization. They see the world through the filter of their past experiences. In the hands of human beings, truth becomes defiled— but could it be any other way?

The *human* element of the religious quest has been recognized by many investigators, but often as a way of saying: "Here, I have explained the religious motivation." "To explain" has most often meant "to explain away." Reductionistic positivists have congratulated themselves on finding the root of the religious sentiment and exposing it for what it is: possessed of human need. If one needs something, so it would seem in the view of these commentators, it cannot be true or real.

The above logic strikes me as dubious at best. To need something, emotionally or physically, does not imply that what will satisfy this need is unreal. Yet this seems to be the logic applied to religion: if one *desires* a sense of cosmic protection, if one *needs* release from moral failure, if one *desires* commitment to that which transcends the purely personal, then that which satisfies these needs is untrue. This point may be illustrated with brief references to the thoughts of Emile Durkheim, Sigmund Freud, Max Weber, and Karl Marx. At least two of these figures have been cited frequently in these pages and the other two are dominant in the literature dealing with religious experience and institutions.

It seems to me that one can acknowledge—indeed, at many points applaud—the insights of these four intellectual giants, and at the same time question the metaphysical conclusions they draw. It is at least logically possible, at the most damning points of their critiques, to still reply: "But so what? Perhaps this is an expression of the truly human, or the way God intended it to be." My point is that whenever social scientists move beyond description and into prescription, they are entering the realm of theology and philosophy.

EMILE DURKHEIM

Let me begin with Durkheim, summarizing a number of the points that I have made in previous chapters.[2] As the reader will recall, Durkheim argued that the object of religious worship is society or, more particularly, the collective beliefs and values of a society (or community). He stated that it is in moments of collective celebration that individuals experience that which they feel to be greater than the sum of the individuals present: namely, the collective conscience of the group. "Collective effervescence"—as it is achieved through song, dance, recitation—elicits feelings of a numinous sort, often identified as the sacred. But rather than the sacred being God, the sacred, for Durkheim, is merely coincident with the collective spirit that binds members into a "moral community."

Except for the philosophically reductionistic side of Durkheim's theory, I am inclined to agree with his description of religious ritual. An important element of worship is collective experience, as generated through rite and ritual. Communal interaction does stimulate the emotions. The feeling of being linked to the community in collective action does give one the experience of power, solidarity. But that is where I want to stop. To explain the social-psychological bases of collective group behavior and the corresponding emotions of individual members of a community says nothing about whether there is a cosmic referent that stands behind the collective ritual.

In my view, it only makes sense that religious feelings are of human origin. Is it not too crudely anthropomorphic to think that feelings of awe and reverence are solely the result of being penetrated by some supernatural lightning, divorced from any particular context? It seems undeniable to me that in collective acts of worship one feels the superordinating presence of the community; one is subdued in the presence of that which is greater than oneself, and the rites of worship are precisely calculated to engender such a feeling. Indeed, worship patterns have evolved because of the ever more finely harmonized ways in which they elicit attunement to the depths of human existence.

SIGMUND FREUD

Freud, a second influential theorist, built his view of religion on a recognition of the inherent weaknesses and frailty of humankind.[3] In childhood one is protected by a father who not only takes care of one's physical needs for food and clothing, but also legislates appropriate moral behavior. There is something comforting in this arrangement: the child feels secure; he or she need only rely on "father" for all provisions, as well as for the boundaries that define moral choice. Freud, of course, argued that in adulthood one misses the sympathetic protection of the father; in fact, life in its unprotected adult state is quite frightening. So consequently, one projects a "heavenly *father*," upon whom one can rely for all one's needs. Such a projection, for Freud, is a sign of weakness, a failure to admit one's predicament in the world.

Again, as in the case of Durkheim, I want to agree with Freud's analysis. Only his conclusions strike me as unwarranted. The father (and I might add, also, the mother) do function in much the way that Freud describes. Adulthood is a frightening experience once one leaves the womb of parental protection and support. One does desire to feel that one is not alone. But, indeed, *who is to say that one is alone?* Freud has certainly not proven that one is. And to say that God, "the father," resembles one's human father is not to invalidate the possibility that God relates to his creation as a father. The great insight Freud offered is that any symbolization of God is rooted in human experience and, hence, one's experience of one's own father may indeed influence the way one conceptualizes God as a father.

MAX WEBER

Likewise Weber, who once described himself as "religiously unmusical," offers important insights which I believe need not threaten the veracity of the religious experience and which may, in fact, deepen our context for appreciating it.[4] As I described in chapter 8, one of Weber's central insights into religious institutions regards their origin and evolution, as specified in his discussion of the "charismatic prophet" and the progressive rationalization and bureaucratization of charisma. Central to Weber's argument is the notion that the charismatic prophet arises in response to social disruption: moments when one belief system has been called into question and another is waiting to be born. In this situation, individuals are ripe for a new proclamation of the truth.

To explain in sociological terms the success of Jesus, Muhammed, and Buddha in gaining a following seems wholly appropriate. However, one may still ask, "But is what they taught and lived *true?*" Religious movements are human enterprises and are regulated by the vicissitudes of history. What else could they be? Furthermore, the charisma of the leader who announces a new way of being is bound to become routinized in the hands of his or her successors. Religious movements are subject to the same laws of social organization as business or political institutions. And they are involved in the same struggles for power, reform, and success. To recognize the human element in institutional religious life is not to invalidate the truth proclamations of the community.

KARL MARX

Karl Marx, another important critic of religion, argued that religion has enslaved individuals rather than liberated them.[5] Religion, he said, has taught suppressed people "servile virtues": temperance, patience, humility. Such virtues dampen the spirit of revolutionary change and pacify individuals into complacent acceptance of their circumstances. Religion, said Marx, has served the interests of the ruling class on two grounds: first, it has been used to deceive the lowest classes into thinking their reward is in heaven rather than on earth; secondly, religion has often justified the position of the rich through a convoluted interpretation of the sovereignty of God—that is, "God established the social order and who am I to tamper with it?"

Marx asserted an important critique of religion, but his view is not necessarily damning to a more positive interpretation of the function of religion. One might argue that almost by definition it is the task of religion to place human circumstances within a larger frame of reference (which has often included the suggestion of immortality and the subsequent amelioration of earthly social inequities). What would religion be if it did not comfort, offer hope, and suggest that temporal existence is not all that meets the eye? Surely a religion that did not inspire confidence in the future and comfort in the present would be a unique species of religion. Indeed, what Marx failed to realize was that he was himself a religious prophet: inspiring hope in the benevolence of the dialectic of history.

SOME TENTATIVE CONCLUSIONS

In downplaying the demonic quality of the four theorists I have mentioned, I do not wish to whitewash the religious enterprise. There are abuses and inadequacies within the institution of the church—and in the religious response of individuals to it—which Durkheim, Freud, Weber, and Marx help to illuminate. But my point is that these four intellectual giants in no way demolish religion; rather, they illuminate its human side. Religious experience is intertwined with the whole of man's social, sexual, political, and intellectual being. There is a danger in extracting the religious response of man from the resolute whole of his personal and social experience. It is much better to acknowledge the complexity of the human organism as a psycho-social unity. Hence, the religious quest proceeds interlocked (and sometimes muddled) with the diverse facets of man's being.

To acknowledge the psycho-social elements of the religious response is simply to acknowledge that religion encompasses the whole range of human experience: the intellectual dimension of religion is complemented by the bodily and physiological elements of human experience, as well as the feeling and emotive aspects of being human. Consequently, to understand the sociological, psychological, and biological correlates of religious experience is not to explain away the experience; rather, it is actually to acknowledge the holistic dynamic of religious experience and commitment.

It seems to me that reductionistic explanations of religious experience often rest on an extremely primitive, if not magical, conception of religion—namely, that religious experience is induced by some nonempirical vapor that emanates from a supernatural force which only those with built-in sensors can perceive. Such a conception presents a religion that is uncorrupted by the "human element," but it also implies a terribly unsophisticated (and, as I said earlier, "primitive") understanding of religion, one which at least few liberal Christians would accept.[6]

Many of the charges against the integrity of religious experience, in fact, may actually be taken as the starting point for a theology of authentic religion. For example: whereas for Freud dependence is an expression of weakness, for Friedrich Schleiermacher it becomes a virtue in his stress upon "absolute dependence" as the core of the religious life.[7] Also, whereas for Marx subservience and meekness are liabilities, in the formidable institution of monasticism, humility, meekness, and ego-loss are the path to enlightenment.[8] Many of the modern ideals of self-sufficiency, autonomy, and independence which implicitly inform the perspective of the modern interpreter of religion have traditionally not been virtues at all.[9] The strength that comes through weakness and the victory that emerges from carrying one's cross are incomprehensible to many individuals blessed with the modern mentality. I am not at all certain that those within the religious context should be shamefaced or attempt to rationalize or cover up these aspects of their tradition.

I am also not certain that those within the religious community should attempt to deny the very human ways in which individuals pursue the religious quest. Many individuals are prompted to question the meaning of life and their place before the Creator during periods of personal bereavement, stress, and crisis.[10] Does such a context for religious reflection point to the inadequacy of those who find God at such moments? Or might one not applaud the fact that human experience is punctuated by moments when people are prompted to consider the acute questions surrounding life, birth, and death? One can perhaps even appreciate the legitimacy of tent meeting revivals and crusades that gather large numbers of people together to hear a speaker address the human condition.[11] Is it weak and inauthentic to be moved by someone who can summon the emotions as he or she speaks about solutions to the trials of life?

BEHAVIORISM

The cynicism of one particular group of social scientific commentators warrants specific examination. For those within the behaviorist school of thought (e.g., Watson, Skinner),[12] one is religious because to be so is "rewarding." All behavior is understood in terms of rewards and punishments (i.e., positive and negative reinforcement); the individual does not consciously shape his or her life so much as he or she responds to what is rewarding or pleasurable. From the behaviorist perspective—with only an occasional exception—the ecstasy of religious experience is parallel in significance to the food pellet dropped to a rat who correctly presses a bar in a Skinner box.

To the extent that religion is discredited by the explanation that religious experience is "rewarding," several things should be said. First, just because someone derives psychic rewards from the activities he or she engages in does not mean the activity is any less worthwhile. Need "truth" be unpleasurable? Or to use a comparable example, if a man says that he enjoys his work, does that make the work any less important or valuable? Second, it is hard to imagine that an intelligent, willful individual would make a choice that he or she did not, on some level, perceive as rewarding. What is important is not whether an activity is rewarding, but whether the activity is good, right, or true. That something is "rewarding" does not, in itself, discredit the authenticity of the choice. Hence, I personally find the oft-cited criticism that "people are religious because it is rewarding to them" a bit dismaying—as if they would be religious for any other reason or as if an unrewarding commitment would somehow be more authentic.

I also fail to understand the attempt by behaviorists to discredit religious convictions and behavior by stating that such choices are conditioned by environmental factors. Indeed, it seems to me that every decision is made within a context and consequently there are always factors which condition the choices one makes. One grows up within a certain environment, one lives at a particular moment in human history, one is of a certain sex, a particular ethnic background, and so forth. All of these factors condition the choices one makes. But a distinction must be made between the terms *condition* and *determine*. The term *condition* refers to the context of experience from which choices are made. The term *determine* points to a necessary result, given certain preordaining factors. All religious choices are made from within a particular context and thereby are conditioned. But it is a matter of philosophical presumption, and not empirical demonstration, to say that religious choices are determined.

FINAL CONCLUSIONS

It seems to me that one of the fundamental shortcomings of many psychologists, sociologists, and anthropologists who analyze religion is their sense of detachment from the travails of human life. From their respective pedestals, they analyze the foibles of the human search for meaning; they spot the inconsistencies; they decry the inadequacies; they note the unanticipated consequences. On one level, their work may stand as a prophetic critique for which the religious community should be grateful. Where would the religious community be today without Freud or Marx to challenge its presumptions? But Freud and Marx must also be held accountable for the cynicism and despair they have bred. They have exploded myths, but what finally have they offered in their place? Are their "myths" superior to what they have replaced? Have they led the human community into a greater experience of truth, joy, hope, justice, and/or corporate responsibility? It would not be easy to answer this question in a few pages or a few volumes. But this much can be asserted: Marxism and psychoanalysis have met with mixed results—as have Christianity, Judaism, and the other historic religions.

Without minimizing the critiques of the classic debunkers of religion, I wish to note what I suspect have been several major oversights among these commentators. Too many social scientists have arrogantly asserted (directly or indirectly) that they hold the key to humanity, that theological insights into the nature of man are primitive, that without religion the New Jerusalem would long ago have come into being.[13] In response to these critics, it must be noted that although religious crusades have killed thousands, Marxian-inspired purges have not been without their body counts. Social utopianism has offered hope to the downtrodden, but let us not forget the impetus lent by religious communities to social reform.[14] Indeed, we may appropriately ask whether we would rather live in B. F. Skinner's Walden II or Calvin's Geneva. Also, we may ask whether psychoanalysis or religious conversion is a more effective modality for changing socially degenerate individuals into productive members of society.

I have no more sympathy for the arrogance of theologians than I do for that of social scientists, but on one level the first

lesson the theologian learns—if he or she is truly a theologian—
is that of human finitude: that he or she is not God. Unfortunately
given the nascent stage of social science, too many sociologists
and psychologists see their ranks as the new incarnation: all knowing, if not potentially all powerful. What they are too often lacking
is an adequate appreciation of human nature—an area that long
has been the forte of the humanistic disciplines of philosophy,
literature, religion.

What many social-scientific observers of religion have a difficult time appreciating, because of their own methodological bias,
is that for those within the religious community, the object of
the religious quest—Truth—is not always to be defined objec-
tively, to be plotted on charts and graphs and placed into laws
of scientific probability.[15] The highest religious traditions have
recognized the *veiled* character of truth: that it is contained in
human stories, in myths; that it is subjective, not objective. Truth
of an ultimate character is more subtle than reinforcement sched-
ules and more demanding in its pursuit than any purely professional commitment. Ultimate Truth is experienced in those
subjective meetings between the "I" and the "Thou."[16] The actual
explanations of these meetings are bound to be conditioned by
an individual's culture, biography, time period, and so forth. But
meetings there seem to be, and for anyone to explain away these
religious moments too quickly through reductionistic reasoning
is to prize quantification over attention to subjective experience.

I have not tried in this chapter to argue that social-scientific
investigations of religion are without their place—indeed, I have
tried to make a case for their value. Rather, I have attempted
to argue for the disciplines concerned with religious experience
to respect each others' boundaries while at the same time profiting
from the breadth of vision that an interdisciplinary approach to
religious experience can afford.

NOTES

1. See the discussion surrounding the so-called naturalistic fallacy in Wilfrid
   Sellars and John Hospers, eds., *Readings in Ethical Theory* (New York: Appleton-
   Century-Crofts, 1952), pp. 63–136.
2. Specifically, see Emile Durkheim, *The Elementary Forms of the Religious Life*, trans.

Joseph Ward Swain (Glencoe, Ill.: Free Press, 1947).

3. The following works by Sigmund Freud bear on this discussion: *Future of an Illusion,* trans. W. D. Robson-Scott, rev. and ed. James Strachey (Garden City, N.Y.: Doubleday, Anchor Books, 1964); *Civilization and Its Discontents,* trans. and ed. James Strachey (New York: W. W. Norton, 1961); *Totem and Taboo,* trans. James Strachey (New York: W. W. Norton, 1950); *Moses and Monotheism,* trans. Katherine Jones (New York: Random House, Vintage Books, 1939).

4. Max Weber, *The Sociology of Religion,* trans. Ephraim Fischoff, with intro. by Talcott Parsons (Boston: Beacon Press, 1963), and *From Max Weber: Essays in Sociology,* ed. and trans. (with intro. by) H. H. Gerth and C. Wright Mills (New York: Oxford University Press, 1958).

5. Karl Marx and Friedrich Engels, *On Religion* (New York: Schocken Books, 1964).

6. Robert Bellah gives a critique of reductionistic approaches to the sociological analysis of religion in *Beyond Belief: Essays on Religion in a Post-Traditional World* (New York: Harper & Row, 1970), pp. 237–259.

7. Friedrich Schleiermacher, *The Christian Faith,* ed. H. R. MacKintosh and J. S. Stewart (Edinburgh: T. and T. Clark, 1928), pp. 12–18 ff.

8. Thomas Merton, *Contemplation in a World of Action,* with intro. by Jean Leclercq (Garden City, N.Y.: Doubleday, 1971).

9. See, for example, Stanford M. Lyman, *The Seven Deadly Sins: Society and Evil* (New York: St. Martin's Press, 1978).

10. See, for example, William James, *The Varieties of Religious Experience: A Study in Human Nature* (New York: Collier Books, 1961), pp. 160–210.

11. See the accounts of conversion which appear in Donald Capps and Walter H. Capps, eds., *The Religious Personality* (Belmont, Calif.: Wadsworth, 1970).

12. B. F. Skinner, *Beyond Freedom and Dignity* (New York: Vintage, 1972).

13. Saint Simon and August Comte are good examples of those who saw religion being replaced by science; see Frank E. Manuel, *The Prophets of Paris* (Cambridge, Mass.: Harvard University Press, 1962).

14. See, for example, Jerald C. Brauer, ed., *The Impact of the Church Upon Its Culture: Reappraisals of the History of Christianity* (Chicago: University of Chicago Press, 1968).

15. Michael Polanyi gives a helpful corrective in *Knowing and Being; Essays,* ed. Marjorie Green (London: Routledge and Kegan Paul, 1969).

16. Martin Buber, *I and Thou,* trans. Walter Kaufmann (New York: Charles Scribner's Sons, 1970).

Epilogue

As I look to the future, I fear that the middle ground between the nonchurchgoing agnostic and the Bible-carrying conservative Christian will be lost. This polarization is unfortunate, because it leaves out the temperate alternative of liberalism, in which one seeks to live within the framework of religious tradition while at the same time interpreting that tradition in terms of a contemporary world view. The liberal Christian is one truly interested in dialogue with those on the forefront of creative achievement in the arts, social sciences, physical and biological sciences—and even business. The liberal Christian is not afraid of culture or of engaging in cultural critique.

I fear that the resurgence of conservative Christianity is not a working of the Spirit so much as a human retreat from the complexities of understanding the Christian faith in terms of a complex world. It is not easy to live as a liberal Christian. One is continually on the edge, the "boundary line" as Tillich so aptly named it. But the danger of the contemporary period is that the boundaries separating the rich and the poor, the educated and the uneducated, developed and less developed countries, are becoming more rigid. The world needs Christians to live on the boundaries that divide peoples and nations and world views. Perhaps those posturing from conservative theologies and a well-defined center can engage in a mediating role. I don't know. I do know, however, that it has been the traditional role of Christian liberalism to stand in the hiatus between polarized factions. This is precisely the root of the necessary instability historically evidenced in liberalism.

My fear is that in the absence of a vital liberal theology, many members of liberal congregations are on their way toward creating a class of formerly religious but now secular humanists. I am not opposed to humanism except when I sense that its proponents know more what they are against than what they are for. They are opposed to authoritarian religion, blind supernaturalism, and culture-despising religion. And so am I. What they have lost—and what the liberal Christian retains—is the mediating institution that would enable them to implement their ideals: the church. Structured community is important—an insight too many humanists see as anathema to their quest for an individualistic freedom. Perhaps that is the dividing line separating liberal Christians from secular humanists; the former believe in the importance of pursuing the fundamental questions of truth and virtue from within a communal context.

Some of the other issues potentially separating secular humanists from liberal Christians—such as the God question—are based on unfortunate misunderstandings. The God I envision is the sustaining Presence of those ultimate values humanists seek. The religion humanists reject as they see Christianity linked with racial prejudice and exploitation is not the "Word of the Lord" that echoes through the prophetic tradition of the Bible. Humanists are rejecting a "straw God," a human substitute for God that liberal Christians heartily join in despising. To be hostile to religion is not to be against the "Word of the Lord" as Jeremiah and Amos and Jesus proclaimed it.

Liberal Christians need the infusion of humanists into their midst, and humanists need the church to aid them in celebrating and actualizing the values for which they stand. In these pages I have attempted to sketch an agenda for liberal Christianity that I believe provides a temperate alternative to both regressive conservatism and secular humanism. We need a rebirth of liberalism as we move ahead into a world in which polarized thinking provides one of the greatest pitfalls.

Index